sparks
1974

Laura Shenton

"Sparks is in its own universe and you don't have to play by the rules.
You can be individual and do something unique and it can still be relevant."

(Russell Mael, as quoted in The Irish News in June 2018)

sparks
1974

Laura Shenton

WP
WYMER
PUBLISHING
Bedford, England

First published in Great Britain in 2020
by Wymer Publishing
www.wymerpublishing.co.uk
Tel: 01234 326691
Wymer Publishing is a trading name of Wymer (UK) Ltd

ISBN: 978-1-912782-44-4

Every effort has been made to trace the copyright holders of the
photographs in this book but some were unreachable. We would
be grateful if the photographers concerned would contact us.

Cover image © Gijsbert Hanekroot / Alamy Stock Photo
Typeset by Andy Bishop / 1016 Sarpsborg.

A catalogue record for this book is available from the British Library.

Contents

Preface

Sparks! What an awesome band! I trust that you will share such bias with me in reading this book. There is so much to say about them in terms of their quirky and powerful music. Currently, there are two biographies out there on the band that document their career overall. I advocate that they are essential reading for any Sparks fan. And thus, this book doesn't seek to be a third biography – that would be futile! Where does this book fit in? Well, 1974 was such a massive year for Sparks, both musically and commercially, and as such, that year alone warrants expansive discussion. 1974 in Sparks' history deserves its own book. So here it is getting one.

On such basis, this book will offer an objective insight into Sparks, their music and the fascinating journey that the band went on; from the early days of struggling to crack America to key moments in them getting their big break in the UK.

In the interests of transparency and context, as author of this book I have no affiliation with Sparks and I have no affiliation with any of the band's associates. I was born in 1988, so quite a while after the band's most prominent achievements. As a result of this, the content of this book is derived from extensive research fuelled by a passion for Sparks' amazing music as well as the hoarding of a range of vintage articles.

On the basis of the latter, if you're looking for a biography that's full of gossip and intensely detailed information on the personal lives of the band members, you won't find that here. Ultimately, that is not information for me to give and inevitably I don't have it anyway (the Mael brothers have done well to avoid the whole celebrity thing; they have done a good job of keeping their personal lives separate from their professional one. Fair play to them). What I do have though is an abundance of research on Sparks and it certainly feels right to collate that here in order to offer an angle on the music and achievements of a band whose musical legacy certainly warrants such exploration.

I have tried to keep speculation and rumours down to an absolute minimum. Whilst I may add my own opinion here and there in the name of being objective, essentially I feel that it is important to refer to fact as much as possible throughout my telling of Sparks' story. As a result, you're going to see a lot of quotes from vintage interviews in this book. I think that's important because there's probably going to come a time where stuff like that gets harder and harder to find. It needs to be collated because Sparks' contribution to music is certainly worthy of such archiving and indeed, discussion.

Chapter One

Sparks And The Importance Of 1974

1974 was a huge year for Sparks. It wasn't the year the band started, but it was the year that, commercially, they got their big break. The story of Sparks in 1974 is one of two brothers, Ron and Russell Mael, who had played with several different bands as part of musically and commercially finding their formula. With a distinctive image and an extent of eccentricity that the British welcomed eagerly, the Californian brothers found their feet with a British tour and the release of the successful albums, *Kimono My House* in May 1974 and *Propaganda* in the November.

1974 was the year that, commercially, things really began to take off for Sparks. Although throughout their fifty-year career their style has varied tremendously and they have explored a range of musical genres, Russell Mael's strong vocal range and distinctive falsetto, along with brother Ron's rhythmic keyboard playing, has been an integral aspect of their sound.

Whilst still on the US club circuit, before they cracked

A very early shot. Ron hadn't perfected his trademark look yet.

the UK, Sparks were always looking to English bands for inspiration. Russell was quoted in *The Scotsman* in September 2005: "Even before we moved to England we thought we were like a British band. We wanted to be The Who and I kind of admired Mick Jagger. We used to play the Whiskey A Go Go in Los Angeles. I would be wheeled on stage in a little ocean liner we made out of wire and papier-mache, waving hello to the crowd of four or even five people. That's when we realised maybe we were not going to be The Who."

It was during the height of glam rock's popularity that Sparks relocated to England. Russell was quoted in the *Daily Mirror* in July 1979: "We are indebted to Britain for supporting us. Our music has always gone down a lot better over here than in the States. Everything there is totally mild and inoffensive. Our music seemed to appeal to only a minority cult."

However, Russell was quoted in *Get Ready To Rock* in December 2007: "Well we never considered ourselves to be a glam band especially as we had done two albums prior to *Kimono My House*. We had kind of already developed our style and put our slant on the music and so the general mould of where we were coming from was already established. So when we became associated with the glam thing we were kind of puzzled, 'cos we had charted our own course before then."

Some people still categorise Sparks as glam rock. *The Irish Independent* asserted in June 2001: "Of the glut of bands to emerge in the early seventies, the one with the closest musical feel to Roxy Music was perhaps Los Angeles duo Ron and Russell Mael whose 1972 album, *A Woofer In Tweeter's Clothing*, was a forerunner for many an art/glam rock group."

Sparks themselves were perhaps not so keen to be categorised. Ron was quoted in *Sounds* in June 1974: "There's no such thing as avant garde or trendiness. I think all those things are in the past." To which Russell added: "That's why I don't think of ourselves as being particularly trendy. We've been involved in it for such a long time we don't consider it being particularly new."

It was advocated in *Melody Maker* in November 1974: "The sound of Sparks is intriguing and imaginative. They blend early production techniques and tricks that worked well to make the records of the fifties and sixties so successful. The band rely on dynamics and rhythmic changes to carry their tunes rather than depend on one basic melody line." True, but that's not to say that melody was secondary to Sparks' music, not even slightly. In fact, one of the reasons that each of their songs are so memorable is that melodically, they are so distinctive.

With their absurd and witty lyrics delivered with Russell's intense falsetto vocals, Sparks came to the attention of the wider public in 1974 with a memorable performance (well, mime!) on *Top Of The Pops* of their breakthrough hit, 'This Town Ain't Big Enough For Both Of Us'. At a time where Queen had not quite reached the height of their campiness (they were on *Top Of The Pops* in 1974 with 'Killer Queen' but hits such as 'I Want To Break Free' had yet to happen), Sparks' eccentricity stood out in a way that propelled them to fame and indeed, popularity, in a big way.

In particular, as much as glam rock had taken off by 1974, a lot of rock music at the time still placed an emphasis on being macho. Essentially, Sparks brought something different to the table. Russell's flamboyant vocals and Ron's aggressive glares into the camera from behind his keyboard were certainly memorable, as was their dress sense − in particular, Ron's Charlie Chaplinesque moustache and slicked back hair. It is rumoured that John Lennon exclaimed, "Christ! There's Hitler on the telly!"

Sparks were different. They stood out, they got the public's attention and most importantly, their music appealed to a wide audience. Still though, Ron's toothbrush moustache was such that a French TV station deemed it too much like Hitler's and consequently banned footage of the band from being shown. Ron was quoted on the matter in *The Independent* in September 2017: "Yes it did have some unfortunate by-products along the way. So I re-thought my facial hair direction. I changed the moustache a bit, it morphed into different things."

In 1974, Sparks' status as a cult band was very much confirmed in the UK. They had several top twenty singles from both their *Kimono My House* and *Propaganda* albums. It was in the first half of 1974 that the media really began taking an interest and were keen to introduce the band to the public. In April 1974, *Melody Maker*'s front page featured a large photo of Russell Mael. They introduced him as follows:

This is Russell Mael, lead singer with the hottest new band in the land — Sparks. The band is rehearsing for its first tour, scheduled to start in late-May and hopefully, coinciding with their first chart success with 'This Town Ain't Big Enough For Both Of Us', Sparks' great debut single for Island Records.

The tour is due to end in mid-June. It will be the band's first British dates with their new line-up. Sparks' new album, meanwhile, will be released on May 17th as a prelude to their tour. Called *Kimono My House*, the album features tracks such as 'Amateur Hour', 'Thank God It's Not Christmas' and 'Talent Is An Asset'.

1974 was an interesting year in terms of the commercial aspect of the music industry. Things were very diverse in terms of how on the one hand, hard rock (and even, to an extent, prog rock) was ticking along as comfortably as it had been in the early seventies. For instance, Deep Purple, Black Sabbath, ELP and Jethro Tull were still churning out successful albums on an almost yearly basis. Glam rock was just about coming to the fore via artists such as Mud and Alvin Stardust. Really, even rock was starting to become very manufactured and certainly less raw than it may have been before (at least in the mainstream). Manufactured bands were pretty common by the mid seventies (when I say manufactured, I'm talking in terms of how bands were designed to appeal to a specific target audience; the music wasn't made with maximum artistic freedom and spontaneity in mind because there were sales and audiences to think about). Basically, in a market where pop bands such as The Osmonds and The Bay City Rollers were very deliberately stylised, Sparks stood out.

Ron and Russell have always maintained that despite Sparks' quirky image, there was never an element of design in how they were presented to the public. Russell was quoted in *The Irish News* in June 2018: "It was always supposed to have been an us vs. them affair. Pop music at its best is when there is a rebellious stance. We don't consciously set out to do that. It's just something inherent in the way we are. We've had a lot of people come up to us through the years and say they appreciated how our music spoke to them, that they could be different and that was cool."

It was considered in *Melody Maker* in July 1974: "So what are Sparks all about? Well, they're an attempt to translate fresh ideas into rock music which is largely unclassifiable. Cool rock fans try to dismiss it as pure pop but Sparks' music, in the words of manager John Hewlett (who was years ahead of his time in John's Children with Marc Bolan) is 'trying to recapture the excitement of the Small Faces and the early Who'. Plain, old fashioned popular music as it used to be before rock's inevitable aging process started. An attempt to show that pop doesn't have to be banal to be commercial. Sparks are an Anglo-American six-piece band who've had one hit single, one hit album and played fifteen dates in seventeen days. That's all. The band is a very, very new one."

So why did some people consider that popular music in Britain was having a bit of a lull in 1974 before Sparks came on the scene? Well, many people were still missing The Beatles. In the many music newspapers of the time that I used to research the content for this book, I came across many articles where music journalists were driving at several points regarding The Beatles: "Will they get back together?" "What's the likelihood?" "Is it a good idea?" etc. Basically, it seems that by 1974, a lot of pop music fans were definitely still missing The Beatles.

It's remarkable really because with the power of hindsight, when you break it down to the basics of the situation, as solo artists by 1974, The Beatles were not particularly active, at least not commercially. John Lennon released the album, *Walls And Bridges*, which was the last of any new material from him for six years. George Harrison's *Dark Horse* album had mostly poor reviews and failed to chart in the UK. Ringo Starr's *Goodnight Vienna* album got to number eight in the US but it was the last of his albums to make the top twenty in the US or indeed the UK. Paul McCartney didn't release an album in 1974.

Now, whilst The Beatles certainly don't signify the absolute holy grail of pop music, the fact is that in 1974, a lot of the music newspapers seemed, in the most extreme instances, to be pining after what was and what was no more. On such basis, some might consider that when Sparks came onto the scene, UK audiences were certainly ready to welcome something that was new and interesting.

With regards to moving to Britain in search of their commercial breakthrough, Ron was quoted in *Beat Instrumental* in August 1974: "One reason that we came here is that we thought it would be easier for us to get good audience reaction. This isn't the kind of universal musical feel where everybody is completely attuned to the music, the barrage papers, the TV shows etc., it's all still a real thing in the States, but here it's in essence. Plus people in England seemed really bored with music."

When asked in the same feature whether he knew if people were bored prior to the arrival of Sparks, Ron was quoted as responding: "Oh no! This is a revelation of the past few months. I don't see it in a negative way, it's just that it's created a situation where there has to be something to do and rock music is what there is to do."

When asked whether it was a calculated move to break in Britain before the States, Russell was quoted in *Beat Instrumental* in August 1974: "No. We were at a point in our careers when we wanted to make a change. We had two albums out in the States and things were just going okay, not really breaking. So we thought we'd just like to split it and change everything around us. We thought we'd like to come to England because we toured here over a year and a half ago. It's not that we thought it would be a pushover, we just wanted a change. England's just another centre for music. I mean, LA's one centre, New York's another... We're going to put the same efforts in at home, we always have."

When asked in the same feature about why it had worked for Sparks in England but not in America, Russell responded: "I don't know, maybe it's just that the time's right. We haven't adjusted the music and said 'right, we've had two albums in the past that weren't that successful, let's do something new!'" Russell was quoted in *LA Weekly* in November 1998: "We had always been huge Anglophiles, and to this day there's a greater acceptance of eccentricity in the music scene there."

The complexity of Sparks' lyrics is such that throughout this book, I'm not going to make an attempt to decipher them — to do so would be futile and misleading because they are so open to interpretation. I want this book to be about what Sparks intended with their music; as one of many fans, it is not my place to speculate on what Sparks' lyrics may or may not mean. Therefore, whilst I will quote from some sources (such as vintage reviews) where attempts have been made at stipulating what a song means, if it hasn't been put out there by the Mael brothers themselves then I would advise caution in such regard (and even then, in the early days of their fame, the Maels delighted in starting a rumour that Doris Day was their mother (she's not!) so make of that what you will!).

Throughout this book, the vast majority of interviews

referred to are ones that featured only Ron and Russell Mael; predominantly, the rest of the 1974 band members were not as prolific in the public eye (at the time and, really, to this present day). It is for this reason that whilst the majority of sources I've referred to in writing this book feature the Mael brothers, it is certainly not my intention to overshadow what the other band members contributed to Sparks in 1974.

In particular, *Kimono My House* and *Propaganda* feature two different line-ups. It's important to take account of that and indeed celebrate it because of course, although writing credits on both albums are attributed to Ron and Russell, the albums are very much band efforts. In such case, it's time to introduce the other musicians. Their names will pop up often in this book so it's important to introduce them here.

Melody Maker featured a biography of Dinky Diamond in July 1974:

> Norman Diamond has been called Dinky
> ever since he was at school and can't rightly
> remember why. Maybe it had something to do
> with his size (about five foot six). He was born
> in Aldershot in December 1950, has three sisters
> and a brother and his family had absolutely no
> musical background but now he's making it and a
> whole coach party of them went to the Rainbow
> to see young Dinky play.
>
> Diamond started playing drums when he was
> thirteen with four or five other classmates at
> school ("In actual fact I started out on bass for

about two weeks. Then I found out I couldn't play bass. No way."). So he tapped around on the drummer's kit and was better ("So I carried on from there. Even though school was up till fifteen, sixteen, I did pretty well at school but no way did I want to stay at school. I wanted to go into the music business whatever happened.").

But he didn't. When he left school he became a paint sprayer at a motor works. All the while he'd carried on playing ("We'd do a weekend in Cornwall and I'd get back at six, seven in the morning and go straight into work and fall asleep there.").

For most of this time Dinky was working with a band called Sky ("That lasted until about two years ago. Then we split up and two of the old band, myself and another singer got together, just a four piece band. He was an amazing singer. We had a deal going through Martin Fordham, the arranger, but there was no front money there. We had all the songs ready to record so Pete Morrison, the singer, got offered a better deal by Danny O'Donovan, who he used to work with before. I haven't seen him since. I'd met John Hewlett before a couple of times when I was with Martin. I didn't know who he was, just knew him by sight. It was a funny coincidence because I'd seen Sparks on *The Old Grey Whistle Test*. I happened to like a couple of things they did and I thought the ideas were good and I just got the rest of the band to do them.").

One evening Hewlett happened to be in the pub they were working ("He came up and then I met Ron and Russ. It was a really funny coincidence."). The transition into Sparks' music wasn't too hard for him ("because the basics of the music are really like a straight thing anyway, they're like a rock 'n' roll thing with just the arrangements that break it up. There's no extra special timings. They're all 4/4, 3/4 and I think one's 5/4. But you don't sit down and think 'ah, that's 3/4', it's just how Ronnie writes it and you realise what time it is in after you've done it.").

Sparks' drummer is also soon to go into print. A piece of flippant fun called Dinky Diamond's Dance Steps has been planned. It came about when he was seen to dance to what were hitherto considered undanceable (sic) songs. At least it'll help all those poor kids on *Top Of The Pops* who couldn't cope with the rhythm and arrangement of 'This Town Ain't Big Enough For Both Of Us'.

To clarify, where the band Sky is mentioned, it is a completely different band to the Sky that came to fame in the late seventies with Francis Monkman on keyboards and with the 1980 hit single, 'Toccata'. Oh and Dinky Diamond's Dance Steps? That was definitely a rumour. It never came to be, not even slightly. It was advocated in *Sounds* in July 1974 that Dinky "still manages to capture the eye as he looks as if he's about to leap over the kit at any moment." Diamond was voted as Drummer Of The Year in a poll held by Premier drums in 1975. He was active with Sparks until when the Mael brothers decided to move back to the US after the 1975 *Indiscreet* album. Sadly, in 2004, Norman "Dinky" Diamond committed suicide. The media reported that overall, it was due to a long-running dispute with difficult neighbours.

Melody Maker featured a biography of Trevor White in July 1974:

> Trevor is short, stocky, fair-haired and does a creditable impression of Dudley Moore. He plays second guitar and has a reputation for lateness and forgetfulness. Trevor's story goes back to when he was twelve and at school around Worcester Park, Sutton ("I was at the same school as manager John Hewlett and we've been best mates ever since.").

> The strands of the White/Sparks relationship start to come together about two and a half years ago. White hadn't played in a band for two or three years but was looking for a new one. Another friend of Hewlett's, Ralph Kimmett, was working in a music publishing office while looking for a band. They got together ("He was Scottish so we went to Scotland."). There they formed Jook ("I had been in a band (the A-Jaes) for years and years and all of a sudden it just started to fade out and went. Then I tried several bands over the years. Got into them, rehearsed for two months and didn't like it or something went wrong and kind of got into a stagnant situation.").

> Jook had a very distinct image and tried to appeal to a specific market. The Nouveau Mod ("It was

mostly John's influence on it. He got his own image bit, I mean he does it all himself and he said, in typical style, 'I think all the band should look like this', it went from there on. Everybody took ideas from everybody else until it did form into an actual image.").

Jook had about three singles out on RCA. In the early stages the company didn't quite know what to do with the group ("They got to it in the end but they didn't really do the initial push. Our earlier singles were the best. If they'd have given us a massive promotion behind the first single it would've been a hit but it was just stuck out as a sort of feeler.").

Their live dates always went well, says Trevor. (They) never played London much until they got a residency at the Edmonton Sundown which they used to pack out. Jook crumbled when the big tour they'd been booked on supporting Sweet was cancelled. It would get them out to the public and they had a single ('Bish Bash Bosh') out to coincide with the tour.

There was nothing fixed for after the tour ("But I mean, I'd known Ron and Russell when they first came over 'cos of John. I was always round his house chatting to Ron and Russ. So I start playing. And that's the best way to be because if you start worrying about the structure of a song then you get a bit fidgety. At the moment I play blues licks 'cos they're the only licks I know. Sparks is just a very fresh rock 'n' roll band. I mean I play in the band and I wouldn't like to have to class it. It's just a very original band, I think.").

White played live with Sparks and on the albums *Propaganda* and *Indiscreet*. He was also with Sparks until the Maels decided to move back to the US in 1975.

Melody Maker featured a biography of Adrian Fisher in July 1974:

Adrian Fisher is a young Spark (twenty-two in August) from Dulwich who plays guitar, takes the occasional solo and revels in a (deliberate and possibly defensive, I think) exaggerated uncouth character. "I'm not embarrassing you, am I?", he'd bellow across a hotel lounge buzzing with hushed conversation.

He plays the young James Dean and like that actor his rebellious nature has a likeable naivety which makes his few real excesses immediately forgivable. Ade started playing guitar after he "got the Bluesbreakers LP. Started at Clapton and I worked me way back from that", a real blues freak, he says. He started in the music business when "I got slung out of school on a Thursday and started at Robert Stigwood's on the Monday. I was the office boy. It was good fun. All yer heroes worked at Stigwood's. It wore off after a while, getting sandwiches for Ginger Baker."

Whenever he had any time spare at Stigwood's, Ade would "skive off down to the kitchen and play bottleneck. Robert Turner heard me playing down there once and when he left Stigwood's to join Island he phoned me up one day about three months later and said, 'there's a geezer here wants a guitar player.'"

The geezer was Andy Fraser in post-Free vacuum. Fraser heard Fisher and after a brief audition Ade joined Fraser's band, Toby.

After Toby split, Fisher sat at home for around seven months. Then he thought of getting another job. He then joined Brush, led by the Irish musician who gave the band its name. In all, Ade was with Brush for eighteen months with a break of two to three months. Finally their management said the band owed them "this incredible amount of money" and that was the end of that.

Fisher did some jamming around ("There was no money or anything. They were just a couple of bands that weren't gonna do anything. I just couldn't stand it. And so I showed up for the auditions with Sparks.").

Did he find it difficult to restrict himself to the fixed structure of Sparks' songs after a career, albeit short, in loose-blowing bands? "We all chip in with arrangement ideas. But he (Ron) doesn't write songs where they've got a verse, chorus, verse, chorus, middle, end and stuff like that. Each song you just have to remember as it comes. I'm a complete blank before they knew me and my guitar playing and everything. They asked me to do it when they first came over. John suggested it. He knew I wouldn't do it then."

Ade's second offer to join Sparks and Ian's first came simultaneously. They went along to a "two-way audition" and if both parties dug what they played then they'd join ("It fitted in straight away. In an hour we did 'Hasta Mañana' and 'This Town' and they were perfect and it sounded great and we thought 'what have we been doing for the last few years?'")

It was advocated in *Sounds* in July 1974: "The next most dynamic character in the band has got to be Adrian Fisher who is an excellent guitarist. Obviously playing someone else's material doesn't give him the opportunity to reveal his full potential, but there's no doubt that he gives a hard edge to the band's sound. Although he's young, he's already had a substantial career playing in Brush Shield's (ex Skid Row) band and also Andy Fraser's short-lived group, Toby."

Fisher played on *Kimono My House* and *Propaganda*, as well as taking part in the tours in between the two albums. After his dismissal from Sparks, in 1977 he joined Mike Patto's band, Boxer, where he recorded the album *Absolutely*. It was released on Epic Records. Other members of the band were ex-Grease Band keyboard player Chris Stainton, ex-Vanilla Fudge/Cactus bassist Tim Bogert, and drummer Eddie Tuduri. Towards the end of the eighties, Fisher moved to Thailand; he worked there as a musician. He passed away (myocardial infarction) after a live performance on 31st March 2000.

Melody Maker featured a biography of Ian Hampton in July 1974:

Ian Hampton plays bass for Sparks, comes from Edinburgh and is nick named Hacker from his Jook days when they'd play soccer in the car park instead of rehearsing.

Ian's story over the past few years runs parallel with Trevor's ever since White and Ralph Kimmett went north to Scotland to form Jook. Ian had done the usual apprenticeship in school bands playing lead guitar. Then "I gave it all up. I went through a phase of playing it and got so pissed off with it I said I'd never touch it again, so I sold all my gear. Until these guys said 'wanna join a band?'; 'love to,' I said. But they didn't want a lead guitarist. They wanted a keyboard player."

Ian's forever joining bands to play an instrument he's never touched before. However, he'd had piano lessons at school and that was more than he had on guitar, which "came off records, sitting in my bedroom. Records of the day. Shadows and all that. Duane Eddy, Chet Atkins."

So after a period sitting on his backside tinkling with the ivories he got the gig with Jook on an instrument he hadn't played before ("Never played bass in me life before when they came. I didn't listen to anybody. There are bass players I respect but I couldn't honestly say there's one that I listened to, to copy").

Ian's "crash course in bass playing" complete, Jook came back to London after spending several fruitless months looking for a Scots drummer and picked up Chris Townson, who'll be remembered for John's Children. Live, says Ian, "We never had a bad gig."

But Jook were the sort of low budget band which would turn up to a gig and do everything themselves while their support bands had roadies, mountains of gear and a vast entourage of hangers-on ("Yeah, I used to do the mixing on stage. I used to stand there with the mixer on me right-hand side — don't know how we survived for so long.").

Inevitably, the end came ("Ralph, the singer and I were up in Scotland doing some promotion. Jook released a single to coincide with the Sweet tour. It was going quite well and receiving more reaction than any of the other singles. I came back on a Saturday. Our manager, John Hewlett, called and said 'are you interested in joining Sparks?' — I thought they were a great group but when it came to it we felt so bad about breaking up the little family we'd been in for a couple of years.").

When Ian came in on bass for Martin Gordon he stuck mostly to the lines recorded on the *Kimono My House* album ("I have to produce what's been done before because that's what the kids want to hear but I've got a free hand on the new stuff. If somebody doesn't like what I play they'll say so. It's no problem.").

Ian Hampton toured with Sparks. He played on *Propaganda* and *Indiscreet*. He was quoted in *Sounds* in July 1974: "I was in Scotland when I heard that Sparks were interested in us. It's been so quick, but I'm really knocked out with the band."

Born in 1954 in Hertfordshire, Martin Gordon took piano lessons in his formative years. It was at jazz college that he started playing bass guitar. Before he joined Sparks, he worked in maritime engineering as a technical author. Having seen Sparks perform on *The Old Grey Whistle Test*, Gordon was aware of Sparks and their connection to Todd Rundgren and was thus responsive when drummer Bob Hurt informed him of an advert in *Melody Maker*. Sparks were looking for a bass player and so Gordon and Hurt went to audition at manager John Hewlett's house. The audition was pretty casual in nature and it took a while before Gordon was convinced that he'd got the job.

Martin Gordon was quoted in *Mojo* in August 2003: "(in June 1973) I saw an advert in *Melody Maker* – 'Wanted: bass player for Sparks. Must be beard-free and exciting'. I'd seen them on *The Old Grey Whistle Test*. Bob Harris dismissed them as 'mock rock' in his whispering sneer. The Mael brothers were living in manager John Hewlett's house in Croydon. I drove down to meet them. Hewlett said to me, without even flinching, 'We're looking for a McCartney to Ron's Lennon.' I thought that sounded interesting. Ron and Russell and I chatted and got on reasonably well, although Ron's moustache seemed ill-advised. A few weeks later I got a call from Russell asking me to bring my bass to Barnet Cricket Club. Chris Townson from Hewlett's other band

Jook was drumming. I think we did 'I Like Girls' and a two-chord bash called 'Girl From Germany'. It went very well and at the end they took me aside and pressed a grubby £10 note into my hand. Thus I knew I was 'official'... There was something of a cultural gap between the Maels and myself. For no clear reason, Russell would show me Polaroids he'd taken of Indian restaurants, but we didn't socialise. We started recording *Kimono My House* that December. During the previous weeks I'd resigned myself to a career as a technical author in maritime engineering, now I was in a pop group. What a hoot."

Chapter Two

Teething Problems

Part of understanding why 1974 was such a big year for Ron and Russell Mael comes from recognising the extent to which things weren't quite working for them commercially in the run up to that year. Upon being asked whether he felt alienated or disillusioned by multiple rejections from record companies in the early days, Russell was quoted in *Sounds* in June 1974: "At first you do and then it got to be the natural thing where you'd be turned down, continually rejected. We took tapes round and they said no and we'd get these stock forms sent back to us which said 'sorry we cannot use your material at present, however in the future if you should have any new material please don't hesitate to send it to us'... We sort of lost sight of ever getting signed."

Having grown up in Pacific Palisades in western Los Angeles, California, Ron and Russell Mael were around during what some consider to have been the golden age of the LA club scene; bands like The Doors, Love and the Standells were regulars at the Whisky A Go Go on Sunset Strip whilst the Beach Boys played afternoon gigs at Teenage Fair. The Mael brothers both went to UCLA. Ron studied cinema and graphic art and younger brother

Coming soon, sooner, soonest: free Python flexi-disc

NEW MUSICAL EXPRESS

WORLD'S
OST
OCK
EERLY

'Velvets
All Star
reunion

ENO, CALE, NICO, AYER
– THE CSN & Y (
DECADENCE? – UNIT
FOR ONCE-OFF G

BBC
film
Wh

GRAHAM BO
KILLED
TRAIN ACCIDE

*Is this town
big enough
for this ma*

ANOTHER DARING EXP
NOPE. JUST A DRIBBLIN
ECSTATIC REVIEW OF
THE SPARKS ALBUM,
AWAITS YOU ON PAGE

Russell studied theatre arts and filmmaking. Although there was also an active folk music scene accessible to the Maels at the time, they were explicit in denouncing their lack of enthusiasm for that genre of music. Their passion for British rock music was to the extent that they declared themselves as being "Anglophiles". Russell was quoted in *Narc* in September 2017: "We've always had a soft spot for the UK, who initially embraced Sparks. We lived in London so we fulfilled our dream of being a British band, and are Anglophiles musically. Ron's earliest listening influences were The Kinks, The Move and above all the early Who..."

It comes across that from a young age, the Mael brothers had a strong sense of their musical preferences. Ron was quoted in *The Guardian* in October 2002: "Our father bought us 'Hound Dog' by Elvis and 'Long Tall Sally' by Little Richard, so those were the first records we owned. I don't know what his inspiration was for doing that. They weren't the kind of records you usually bought as educational tools for your child... We detested folk music because it was cerebral and sedate and we had no time for that, but the Byrds were okay because they electrified it and they had English hairstyles."

Ron was quoted in *The Times Magazine* in March 2003: "We grew up in Venice, California. Right now it's being gentrified but when we were growing up it was more middle and lower class, It's odd, people here (UK) consider us to be from well-to-do backgrounds, but we're really not at all. Our father was a graphic illustrator at *The Hollywood Citizen News*, and mother did some teaching, but there was no one involved in music or performing. I had always bought records — 45s. I loved pop music and at the same time I was forced to take piano lessons between the ages of six and eleven, something like that. I stopped because I liked sports a lot more. But I never made the connection between real pop music and me. There was no plan to go into it, ever. I loved Elvis, and our father had bought us 'Hound Dog' and 'Don't Be Cruel'. And Little Richard I thought was unbelievable. But there was no thought of actually doing those things, being in a band, because we were just two guys from Venice, California."

Russell was quoted in the same feature: "I was in the school choir, but that was simply because you had to do something extracurricular. I think it was quite a bit later on, when I saw English groups coming to play in Los Angeles — The Who, The Rolling Stones — that I thought it might be fun. Our mother drove us to Las Vegas to see the Beatles." To which Ron was quoted: "We also saw them at the Hollywood Bowl for one of their twenty-five-minute concerts. We were sitting there with these little kids — but our mum thought it was worth it. It was mass hysteria, you couldn't hear anything."

Music is something that probably came very naturally, whether it was aspired to or not. Ron was quoted in *Sounds* in June 1974: "For me, there's no such thing as relaxation, which is bad 'cause I wish there was so I could lay out on a beach for a week and not think about anything. But all of that time all of these lyrics and tunes would be flying through my head. So I'm just, for better or worse, really trapped by it." To which Russell was quoted: "Yeah, I'm in a similar situation. Maybe I could relax for five minutes more — but only five minutes."

Ron was quoted in *Sounds* in December 1974: "Originally it (music) was to become a part of the gang, to impress other people, to impress girls, and it was the thing to impress friends as well. It was something more natural in a way, you were always hearing records, you were always surrounded by music. Friday night there were dances and at the beach there was a radio. It was exactly the same thing as playing in a football team. It was the only way to be a hero at that certain time. You couldn't be a hero by going into the army because it was starting to turn the other way – there weren't many other ways. That was the only way to be a hero and not work hard at it."

Spending their formative years in the Pacific Palisades during the sixties, the Mael brothers had a seemingly all-American childhood that included going to the beach and playing sports. Russell was the quarterback of the Palisades High School football team. He was quoted in *LA Weekly* in November 2018: "It's hard to believe I was once a football player, especially looking at my stature now. We liked playing baseball and football. I was on the high school football team for three years. Ron played at Uni High because Palisades High hadn't opened yet... It was so contradictory being part of that beach culture, but we were also Anglophiles. There was a conflict in us. We were born in Los Angeles, but we also gravitated toward the British scene. We stood out dress-wise, trying to emulate the British bands. It was all kind of a weird hodgepodge. Despite living in the Palisades, we weren't from a wealthy family."

Ron was quoted: "It was a different kind of culture. We were attuned to the beach culture. It was a kind of religion, going to the beach all day, surfing and playing volleyball. We were looking to England (for music), but equally there were bands here in Los Angeles reflecting our culture... We always bought the British versions of albums. We'd go to the Whisky A Go Go and see The Move or Tyrannosaurus Rex when it was just a duo. It was a whole different world to us. Image wasn't a concern for the (local hippie) bands. We were supporting Little Feat and Johnny Winter early on but we had no connection to those bands musically. The Whisky, against any logic, would book us even when we weren't drawing. They would keep having us back."

Ron was quoted of the bands he saw during the sixties in *Diffuser* in September 2017: "Oh yeah, we saw the Who, the Move at the Whisky a Go Go, we saw all the British bands, very few of the American bands. We were fortunate. We saw people like Tyrannosaurus Rex, pre-T. Rex, it was just this world we really wanted to be a part of... We played at the Whisky a Go Go often. That was our main, maybe only place really. They really liked us there, so they would have us back, despite our not having a massive following."

Ron was quoted in *Record Collector* in July 2003: "There was such an LA style at the time, so we thought we were an English band. We kind of pretended that we were an English band – that alone offended most of the audience!"

When the Mael brothers made their very first music recording, they did so under the name of Urban Renewal Project. They recorded four tracks with some friends, a married couple – Fred and Ronna Frank – at Hollywood's Fidelity Recording Studios in January 1967. The songs were pressed onto two acetates. The only one of the four songs to get any kind of release was called 'Computer Girl'. It was featured on a CD that came with a Sparks Japanese release in 2006. More recently (and indeed accessibly!), the track was released in 2019 as part of the *Past Tense* greatest hits album.

Halfnelson were formed in 1968 and whilst the music business overall couldn't quite see the appeal of them, one Todd Rundgren persuaded Albert Grossman to sign the band to his new Bearsville label. Even in the days when the Maels went by the name of Halfnelson and were struggling to crack the US market, Grossman was a powerful ally to have in the music business. Born in Chicago in 1926 to a family of Russian Jewish ancestry, Grossman had quit his career with the Chicago Housing Authority in order to manage bands in the folk music scene. Grossman set up a club in Chicago. He called it the Gate Of Horn and expanded by teaming up with managements involved with the Newport Jazz Festival. Together, they set up the Newport Folk Festival. Although Grossman began his music management career in folk music, by the sixties he was certainly not restricted to that one genre and was a major player with artists including The Band, Bob Dylan and Janis Joplin, as well as Todd Rundgren.

It was in 1969 that Grossman opened the Bearsville recording studios. Situated in upstate New York, the Bearsville label was started the following year. As a record label, Bearsville were in an interesting situation because on the one hand they were set up independently but equally they were under the umbrella of Warner Brothers. Halfnelson signed to Bearsville 1970.

When asked "How did Todd Rundgren get involved to produce the first album?", Russell was quoted in *Diffuser* in September 2017: "We sent our original demos to everybody and got either no response or one of those 'we really enjoyed your material, however, at this time we are unable to sign you but if you have any new material in the future, do not hesitate to send it to us' kind of letters. We got those from everybody, then one last person who was sent the material was Todd Rundgren, and it was just like one hundred and eighty degrees from everybody else that had a position to sign us. He had his label Bearsville, which was him and Albert Grossman. The two of them were really passionate about what we were doing. It was kind of shocking that they saw something unique and special in what we were doing when no one else was able to see that same thing.

We owe Todd a big bit of gratitude."

Ron was quoted in the same feature: "He saw that as a strength, where everybody else saw that as a weakness. Everybody wants to find where you fit in with things, but Todd, because he saw that we weren't fitting in with everything, that's what appealed to him. He never tried to sand down the edges."

Prior to being signed to Bearsville, Halfnelson were considerably experimental in their approach to making music. Russell was quoted in *Record Collector* in July 2003: "Earle was really talented at recording, just on a reel-to-reel tape player. We could do whatever we wanted − playing things backwards, speeding-up vocals. It was a very different attitude to a lot of LA bands at that time. Mostly, new bands went out and played their stuff in front of a public and assessed how it faired." To which Ron was quoted: "We were doing things like sampling one note from a classical record − long before 'sampling' was even a term. We didn't have to worry about what anyone thought, because no one was hearing it. We were just doing what we thought sounded cool."

Ron was quoted in *Sounds* in June 1974: "One reason why we were hated even more than we might have been is because we just concentrated on recording. Technically out of the three of us, Earle was always good and we would just spend days and days making little tapes, overdubbing and overdubbing on a little recorder that he hooked up so we could overdub on it. There were some incredible sounding tapes that were done just purely synthetically and they sounded really synthetic. We had trouble getting signed at first because our stuff sounded a little too, er, studio. Eventually we sent a tape to Todd Rundgren and he liked what he heard, his girlfriend liked what she heard and I think she had a big hand in getting us signed."

Halfnelson's eponymous debut album was released in 1971 and it featured the following band line-up: brothers Earle Mankey and James Mankey on guitar and bass respectively and Harley Feinstein on drums. The record was produced by Todd Rundgren. It sold poorly. It was re-issued as Sparks in 1972 when the band changed their name. The re-issue carried the single, 'Wonder Girl', but It was only a minor hit and commercially, was very slight compared to what was to become the 1974 version of Sparks.

Todd Rundgren was quoted in *Classic Rock* in October 2016: "At the time I worked with them they were this weird band from LA who were called Halfnelson. While they must have had some commercial influences on their first album, it was one of the strangest projects I've been involved in. Essentially the core of the band was two pairs of brothers – the Maels and Mankeys – and another guy (Harvey Feinstein on drums). There seemed to be a lack of focus in the group when I was working with them. They wanted to produce this strange music. The Mael brothers had this highly developed image thing going but it seemed the rest of the band was more committed to playing. The stuff they had been writing up until then was way out of the mainstream, and they wanted to become a little more commercial. It was obvious that Ron was doing this kind of Chaplinesque thing; he was like a silent movie, and he never said anything."

Russell was quoted in *Get Ready To Rock* in December 2007: "Early on we thought that what we were doing was something unique, and that the term rock wasn't essential to what we were doing. It was just we had a special way or viewpoint of pop music and music in general. So we always had the kind of aspiration not to be going down the straight and narrow path of pop music."

There aren't many articles around that feature the

Mael brothers from their Halfnelson days (yep, before the name Sparks was even a thing!), but one such feature was written about Halfnelson in *Sounds* in October 1970. It is a vital insight into how the Mael brothers and their music were perceived before stardom and their eccentric image informed what was written about them. The article was titled, "Half Nelson (sic). Ahead Of Their Time?":

> It's not too difficult to "discover" groups who are just beginning long and shiny careers, getting pick singles, making smash appearances, opening one-nighters, releasing incredible first albums. But how about discovering a group that is a total failure?
>
> So, presenting for your consideration — Half Nelson Who?
>
> Half Nelson is a Los Angeles based quintet that every record company seems to love, but that no one will buy. The group consists of two sets of brothers (Russ Mael on lead vocals and his brother Ron on organ, and Earle Mankey on lead guitar with his brother Jim on bass) and drummer Harley Feinstein.
>
> They have been more or less together for two years and haven't made a cent, except once when Earle found a dime under the organ. The group practices in a North Hollywood plant that manufactures bunk beds for dogs — hence their home away from home has become Doggie Bunk Bed Factory. We haven't been out of this room in two years except to go to McDonald's for something to eat," says Russ.

In fact, one trip to the hamburger stand almost made it for Half Nelson. "There was this lady in a mink coat and her poodle was eating our french fries," they relate. "She wanted to know if we wanted to sign with her husband's record company. We were kind of suspicious, but we knew she was legit when she showed us a picture of her husband with Tiny Tim. We took her back to our manager's house and she had a terrible fight with his girlfriend. That ended that. Our bass player had to take her home. Then we found out that her husband's name was 'Big Louie' — he had some rather unsavoury connections. But she promised us all the free copies of our album that we wanted."

About the album — Michael Burns, the group's optimistic manager, gathered up the cash to make an album — one that no one will buy. It's called *A Woofer In Tweeter's Clothing* and the cover shows a surfer riding the Eifel Tower on a heavy.

When will the bubble burst, Half Nelson wants to know? It isn't that the group is inept. They're just weird. Their music is unlike anything happening today — which is probably one reason no one will take a chance and sign them.

But they are a gas to watch because they are so funny. Which is probably one reason everyone likes them so much. They are becoming underground favourites of the recording company underground.

"Everyone at Warner's liked us except the A and R people," they sigh, "And Russ Regan of UNI records said Half Nelson is two years ahead of its time. We've managed to get two guys fired. One guy believed in us and his company wouldn't sign us so he was fired and the other guy never even heard us and he got fired."

The feature continued:

The only way to describe them musically is to put them somewhere between The Kinks and the Bonzo Dog Band — closer to The Kinks musically, and they are, well, weird. In other words, without consciously trying, their sound and manner is very English. They could be an immensely popular performing band. They would do a second album but the lack of paying gigs has rather put the bite on the old equipment — for the first LP they used a piece of cardboard and a mallet for a bass drum.

But they're used to adversity. Russ and Ron used to lead a group called the Urban Renewal Project. Unfortunately, they didn't qualify for state aid. They played at the Los Angeles Sports Arena Battle of the Bands with the whole group going through one amplifier. The guitar player's wife ended up being the drummer. They had a snare drum.

"We were edged out by a couple of other bands," they sigh. "Taj Mahal was there but he lost too. We didn't have a bass, so we used a $20 guitar and told the bass player, who didn't know how

to play bass anyway, to pick low notes. He froze.
At another Battle of the Bands at the YMCA,
there were only two groups. The other group
kept pulling out our cords. We played our most
obnoxious song in retaliation and they closed
the curtain on us. We kept on playing and noticed
something was wrong. We were all playing in
different keys. Then we played at an industrial
design conference at UCLA. All these straight
people wanted a rock band, but the only time we
could play was when they were eating."

Ron and Russ and their trusty amp found Earle at
UCLA from a note pinned up on a bulletin board.
They found Harley by pinning up a little pink note
at Ace Music store in Santa Monica. Their previous
drummer had been rock critic John Mendleson
but he didn't exactly work out. They added Earle's
brother Jim on bass. Says Earle, "Jim is a better
guitar player than I'd ever hope to be but he's
playing bass because I'm bigger."

"The group is going to make it," says a smiling
manager Michael, "I'm tired of being called a
lunatic."

They have a gig coming up at a local club — no
money for them. In fact, it's going to put them
even more in the red because they have to rent
equipment. "We're hoping for a miracle," they sigh.
Right...

Bloody hell! What an article! If it wasn't so tragic it would be funny. There is certainly no denying the farcical nature of some of the band's experiences. Still though, whilst there is an element of humour present because I read the feature with the knowledge of hindsight, it still must have been a painful experience for a group of young musicians who were probably trying their best. They must have really wanted to make a go of things if they were willing to go into debt over it for such a number of years. Knowing what became of the Mael brothers, and ultimately Sparks, there's a lesson there: never give up. And the record company bods who first believed in Halfnelson and got fired for doing so? Damn! It seems like the music industry missed an opportunity with those guys. I hope they had the last laugh somewhere along the line! On the other hand, would the Sparks as we know it have come to be if it wasn't for the teething problems that the Mael brothers experienced at the start of their career? Maybe it's one of those "everything happens for a reason" kind of things. Who knows?!

Notably, *A Woofer In Tweeter's Clothing* was mentioned as early as 1970, despite the fact that this was actually used as the title for Sparks' second album that was released in 1973. It's obviously the case that the idea for the name of such an album existed before the actual album came to be in 1973. However, there are some fan sites that have blogged about an album that exists by the name of *A Woofer In Tweeter's Clothing* that was released in 1970 (possibly 1971) on such a small scale that it wasn't even catalogued as such. Essentially, what we have here is either a) it's the real deal and it hasn't been confirmed as such by a reliable source to this day or b) it's a flipping good hoax because photographs exist of such a record. I've opted to be candid in this book about what isn't known on such front; the information is of note, particularly in view of the *Sounds* article from October 1970, but equally, the facts remain unconfirmed.

Although Sparks' second album on Bearsville, *A Woofer In Tweeter's Clothing* — released in February 1973 — didn't make an impact in the charts in the US or the UK, it did at least get the ball rolling to an extent. The album led to a tour of the UK. In playing at the Marquee Club in London, the Mael brothers were able to get the attention of people with industry influence. Really, in the early seventies, it's plausible that the music industry was more forgiving than it is nowadays; after a few commercially weak records, it didn't necessarily mean that it was over for a band. Ron was quoted in *Loud And Quiet* in July 2018: "We're really fortunate, because if we were coming up now there's no way we'd have more than one album. It didn't matter for us on the first couple of albums if they only sold five thousand copies — (the label etc.) would stick with us and we are appreciative of those people. Now everybody has to do very well very quickly or your opportunity is gone and the next person is moving in."

It depends where your musical tastes sit but there are so many high profile bands who, at the peak of their careers in the seventies, had one or two albums behind them that were musically acclaimed but not commercially significant at the time of release (for example, Deep Purple, Jethro Tull, Supertramp, Queen). It's difficult to imagine now but a lot of bands who are considered by many to be iconic today may not have been given the chance to grow in today's music industry where there is a greater demand on artists to have immediate success at the risk of losing their industry support. Russell was quoted saying of their second Bearsville album in the *Newark Advocate* in July 1975: "We thought of a boring name. Sparks, and put a boring photo of us on the front of the second album – *A Woofer in Tweeter's Clothing* – and proved it wasn't in the name. Nothing happened with that record either."

It was reported in *Beat Instrumental* in August 1974 as Sparks were introduced at the beginning of an interview:

Sparks are new and the new always seem to have an amazing background these days. Were the gullible media to believe the suggestions about the frontmen, the Mael brothers, it would seem that two new superstars kindly decided to give Britain the honour of allowing their discovery to be made in her territories.

The truth is very different. Sparks broke in quite a calculated way. Island Records is one of the most powerful promotional machines in the record industry. This own track record is so good that a new Island signing is in itself of interest because the stoical and unusually immovable Muff Winwood (remember him) and the less obvious although totally autocratic shop owner Chris Blackwell think very carefully before saying yes.

So the buzz went out about Sparks. We are led to believe that Sparks started the ball rolling when they toured here in October 1972, but in reality they failed to make any impression and anyway, they were a different band – only the Mael brothers being common to both.

Roxy Music enjoyed the "Island Buzz" before they broke, and Sparks rode on a similar wave. This is not intended to be derogatory to their music, today, which is almost incidental to the method used in exposing it. The brothers are really nice. They seem deliberately ambiguous about their sexuality in their opposing images and their privileged US backgrounds (child TV models, UCLA students in LA) lessen the impact of their success.

Nevertheless, the brothers are still early enough in the business of handling interviews not to have got beyond a limited selection of glib answers to the most obvious of questions. From time to time I may be unable to decipher my tape accurately, and if I accidentally attribute a quote to Ron when Russ uttered, or vice versa, I apologise.

The reporter almost sounds frustrated that Ron and Russ were not excessively candid people to interview. In 1974 and throughout Sparks' career, many journalists and fans have expressed similar frustrations. Fairly enough though, Sparks are known for their music and whilst their eccentric image is certainly attention grabbing, if they choose to have a firm boundary between who they are as musicians and who they are in their own time, then power to them really. Also, where the journalist admits that he may have got Ron and Russell mixed up at times, in every instance that I quote from *Beat Instrumental* in this book, of course, the same applies.

For everyone who wasn't convinced by Halfnelson/early Sparks, there were people who did believe in them. In 1972,

Music Scene ran a series of features on bands who they were expecting to break big commercially. In November 1972, the publication ran a feature on Sparks. The subheading stated that it was "number one in a new series where a *Music Scene* writer spotlights a band he tips for success."

As with the article from *Sounds* in October 1970, it is an excellent example of where Sparks were at with things prior to their more prolific days on Island:

> There's something definitely mimsy (sic) or even fey about Sparks' music which is complemented by the somewhat precious stage act. Sparks, you see, are one of those West Coast American bands who have picked up on some of the better English bands, listened to the music, steeped themselves in it and emerged with a presentation that is centred somewhere around Goose Bay (or wherever halfway between the UK and the US really is).

> Focal point of the band is singer Russ Mael whose eyes glisten in the darkness of a club and who cavorts around the stage using his hips and arms and hands to emphasise points in a song. His brother, Ronnie, plays organ and it is on Ronnie that a lot of attention is being focussed. For Ronnie looks like Charlie Chaplin with a dash of Adolf Hitler thrown in. When he's playing, he lets his face, and particularly his eyes, speak for him. I am always waiting for the laser beams to come out of those penetrating eyes.

> It was not unnatural then, that the brothers Mael were the ones selected to meet me at WEA's

offices near Centre Point. We discussed first the group's beginnings, Russ and Ronnie taking it in turns to narrate.

Russ: "We started about five and a half years ago with just Ronnie and me looking for a third member. We were at the University of California in Los Angeles where we met Earle Mankey (guitar) who was looking for a band to join. For two years there were just three of us."

Ronnie: "It took us two years to realise we didn't have bass or drums and that's maybe why we didn't hit off too well."

Russ: "We didn't do anything live, we just made tapes and elaborate presentations for record companies. We got through twelve albums that way, but every time we got to the guy just below the one who signs the contracts, he got fired for wanting to sign a group like us!"

The feature continued:

Finally, the band, at this stage called Half Nelson (sic), decided it was time to get on the road. So they roped in Earle's brother, Jim, on bass and Harley Feinstein on drums.

The band was ready for the world, but was the world ready for the band? "We did 'Give It To Me' by the Troggs and Earle's brother almost left because of that," Ronnie recalled, Russ taking over with: "We showcased one British rock song to show that in Los Angeles we really knew about

Ron in Hilversum, Netherlands, 1974 with that trademark look.

(Gijsbert Hanekroot / Alamy Stock Photo)

British groups. It was hard getting jobs playing live because nobody wanted to hear that sort of thing."

Things weren't that bad, but they could've been a lot better. England, it was decided, was to be the next nut to attempt to crack and Sparks, as they had since become, arrived here in November for an indefinite period. "We felt that with our kind of stuff there would be more of a reaction in England and we could work the 'grass is greener' syndrome and return to America after a smash tour of twenty-eight dates in thirty days. There's a lot of guys walking round Hollywood Boulevard trying to look like they're on King's Road. An English group can open its mouth in Los Angeles and go 'Ta' and everyone goes crazy."

But if Sparks weren't working all that much back home, how did they manage to survive? "I was an ice cream man for two days," Ronnie confessed with the trace of a snigger, "I tend to romanticise jobs. We all had various jobs on the outside." Russ: "We managed to find some people along the way who would throw in some money and they're all waiting for something to happen to Sparks, then there'll be eleven Sparks bootleg albums coming out. We took lots of philosophy classes so that though we weren't making money, we could justify it!" And Ronnie: "There were the two English invasions and since then nothing's come along that had that fresh naivety about it, pardon my German. Everything's more cynical now, there was much more of a singles approach to the music business then."

Russ and Ronnie insist that there's nothing contrived about the band's act, preferring to describe it as "a development" of what went before. Everybody on stage is a slight exaggeration of what they are in real life, they add. "It isn't like we'd been to the planet Xenon, like we keep reading in the British press," Ronnie joked, "it's just magnified from playing different kinds of jobs, Mormon dances and things like that — you sit there and think 'what on earth are we doing playing a Mormon dance of all things?'"

Ronnie, who writes most of the songs, claims that he spends a lot of time walking round supermarkets where he finds influences for lyrics. See what I mean about a different band? "We think our songs are just bizarre, but they're just songs," says Russ, "the singing lacks a certain soulful quality and people think it's a change because there aren't enough Wimpy rock singers around."

Wimpy rock singers? "Yes, you know, Wimpy rock singers," he stressed. Oh well. "We never just went on and played, we always made it visual," Russ went on, "the whole rock and roll thing is boring, I would rather go to a good movie."

Whether or not Ron was joking about getting inspiration for lyrics by walking around supermarkets, it cracked me up as I transcribed the article. Funny guy, even before the fame and unrelenting media interest became part of day to day life for the band in 1974. From the 1972 article, it's clear that Sparks had come a very long way from the grim struggles of 1970. The power of persistence and dedication. Greater achievements were definitely just around the corner.

Sparks' fan club fizzles out

THIS WEEK brings another tale of woe about fan clubs. It's the Sparks' club this time.

Lindsay Warren, a reader in Chepstow, phones us in desperation. She sent £1 in June for membership of the club and since then has written four letters asking when she would see something for her money. Until now she has had no reply from the club, not even an acknowledgement. When the club started in this country there were glowing reports on how it was handled — the quarterly booklets produced were informative, attractive and well worth the fans' subscription money.

Joseph Fleury who has been running the club since its inception started by replying personally to every letter.

But there is a limit to the amount of fan mail one person can handle and when the membership grew past the 1,000 mark, it became impossible to deal with it efficiently. Added to this, Mr. Flewy spent part of the Summer in the States and during his absence the fan mail was completely unattended.

The backlog is being cleared now and a mailing is due to go out within the next two weeks.

September 28, 1974

THE LIGHTNING fast rise to fame for Sparks has been quite an enigma. I mean their debut hit single wasn't instantly appealing in a commercial sense and their excellent "Kimono My House" album has been riding high in the charts since its release, which means they are no one hit wonders.

SUICIDAL PROPAGANDA

**Interview:
Pete Makowski**

Chapter Three

Kimono My House

It was in 1973 that Ron and Russell Mael relocated to England. Commercially, they just weren't getting the breaks they needed in the States. Besides, it made sense to move to England because the Mael brothers were already certain of their interest in all things English. Russell was quoted in *Get Ready To Rock* in December 2007: "The most important thing for us has always been what we are doing musically so in that sense England did fulfil our vision of what we thought it was going to be in terms of the music scene. The music scene over there has always been far more vibrant than what it is in LA. So we got drawn into this diverse scene and it led to our album being such a success at the time."

It's fascinating to consider that had Sparks have been from, say, London, their oddball image may have just been put down to the fact that they were British and eccentric as part of that. If Sparks were British, it may have been easy for people to think of their oddball image in terms of "oh, those British! Aren't they quirky?" (it certainly didn't do David Bowie any harm!).

But the fact is that coming from Los Angeles, a cool

and laidback place, Sparks were outsiders there and in a way, they were outsiders when they came to Britain too. The important thing, however, is that they were welcomed. Besides, Sparks' oddball image is very much part of their appeal, both musically and in terms of their image. Ron was quoted in *Diffuser* in September 2017: "We were really fortunate. The strange thing was, our passion for music always was inspired by the British bands, so when we kind of became a transplanted version of that, it was a dream come true for us. We felt like we fit in really naturally, where in Los Angeles we felt like fish out of water."

With two albums behind them that had barely touched the bottom of the charts in the US, when Island Records called from the UK, it was a big deal. They offered Ron and Russell a deal to come to London alone and build a new line-up of the band. Russell was quoted in *The Scotsman* in September 2005: "We were so naive that we didn't think of the consequences. We sold everything we had — 'no reasonable offer refused' — and moved to England, not knowing what to do if it hadn't worked. Fortunately Ron had a wet Sunday afternoon in Clapham Junction and wrote 'This Town'." On 22nd November 1973, Sparks signed a contract with Island Records stipulating that four albums would be made. The contract was signed by Ron Mael, Russell Mael, Martin Gordon, Adrian Fisher, Dinky Diamond and (of Island Records) David Betteridge.

When asked when it was that he wrote the material for *Kimono My House*, Ron was quoted in *Sounds* in June 1974: "Last summer we were here (UK) and it was the combination of really nice weather plus the fact we were here almost as tourists so we didn't get too much time and after that time the whole pace was accelerated, so as we got closer to the recording session more songs were written. We don't, well we can't, write to order. We're not really songsmiths so we were fortunate that in our whole history whenever we needed songs this great bolt of lightning comes out of the skies and strikes us and a song is in the can. That's the way it will continue to happen."

Being signed to Island was an excellent opportunity for Sparks. The record label already had a rich history behind it. It was formed by Chris Blackwell in 1959 in Jamaica before being relocated to the UK three years later. In the UK, Island's initial remit was embedded in making Jamaican music available to immigrant communities. By 1964 though, Blackwell began to sign music with wider commercial potential onto Philips Records (well, Fontana, which was a subsidiary of Philips Records). Blackwell produced 'My Boy Lollipop' by Millie Small. Whilst it featured a Jamaican ska beat, it was an international hit. Also on the label were a number of hits by the Spencer Davis Group, featuring one Stevie Winwood (a renowned singer, he went on to have a career in Traffic, Blind Faith and Go).

'My Boy Lollipop' is an important part in the story of how Island Records grew to the point that it was able to add a wider range of artists to its portfolio. Blackwell had purchased an earlier version of the song by a different artist back in 1959, and finding a copy in his archives in 1963, he was responsible for Millie Small's version. It got to number two in the UK and the US. It sold six million records worldwide and this largely accounted for what then became possible for Blackwell to do with Island Records.

In 1967, Blackwell and his business partner, David Betteridge, decided that Island would be based in London. The move to the creative community in Notting Hill was the perfect setting for the company. It enabled them to focus their marketing towards a young rock album buying audience. Muff Winwood's new group, Traffic, was chosen to be the flagship group on Island's new pink label whilst American producer Joe Boyd contributed music from folk artists Nick Drake and Fairport Convention. As a means of clarifying Island's intended direction, ironically perhaps, most Jamaican artists were signed on a subsidiary label — Trojan Records, which was run by Lee Gopthal at a separate location. By the early seventies, with Roxy Music and Free on Island Records, it solidified the independent label as being a vital contributor to the music scene in the UK. As part of this, it was plausibly a factor in Chris Blackwell being in a good position for promoting albums by Bob Marley to a wider audience.

Chris Blackwell was quoted in *The Independent* in July 2008: "I didn't know anything about the record business, but I was a big fan of music, particularly jazz. I started with a jazz act: I recorded them, got it mastered and manufactured and took the records around myself. That's how it was when I came to England in 1962 too. I'd drive around the parts of London where all the Jamaicans lived and deal with the retailers. It was the personal relationship with all those shops that gave me the shot to build up the early part of Island Records. When I started, there was EMI and Decca, and they had ninety-five per cent of the market share. Then there was Philips and Pye, so there was about one and a half per cent for the independents. Over the years, the majors retreated little by little and the independents built up: ourselves and Chrysalis and Virgin and others had really quite a lot of clout."

Sparks were financed by Island before things started taking off commercially. Russell was quoted in *Beat Instrumental* in August 1974: "Island has been really good in that respect. We got everything as an advance."

Pete Makowski reported in *Sounds* in June 1974: "They've written hits like 'Whippings and Apologies' and 'Nothing Is Sacred' but that was with the old line-up." Ron was quoted in the same feature: "People always had trouble classifying what we were doing at that time, it's now worked to our advantage."

Kimono My House was Sparks' third album overall and their first on Island. The line-up from the Bearsville days was no more and a new British band formed the new version. Earle Mankey, Jim Mankey and Harley Feinstein were left behind in favour of the British line-up of Martin Gordon, Adrian Fisher and Norman "Dinky" Diamond on drums. *Kimono My House* was produced by Muff Winwood but the Mael brothers' first choice of producer was actually Roy Wood.

With regards to producers, Russell was quoted in *Diffuser* in September 2017: "Roy Wood was actually the first name we thought of when we did the *Kimono My House* album. We were signed to Island to work with Muff Winwood, and he was friends with Roy, because they're both from Birmingham, so he approached him on our behalf. We really loved the Move, and in particular Roy Wood we thought was amazing. I don't remember the circumstances, but he wasn't able to do the project, obviously, then Muff just said, 'I should just do it' and we thought, 'Well he's the brother of Stevie Winwood and the bass player from the Spencer Davis Group, so how great is that?' So we said, 'Yeah, you do it.'"

John Hewlett was satisfied that the rest of the band were an excellent choice in supporting the Mael brothers to work at their very best. The line-up featured on *Kimono My House* is Martin Gordon on bass, Adrian Fisher on guitar and Dinky Diamond on drums (as well as castanets). Producer

Muff Winwood considered it to be the case that the rest of the band complemented Ron and Russell well because they added a strong element of hard rock in contrast to Ron's ideas and Russell falsetto vocals. Essentially, the rest of the band kept the Mael brothers grounded and it could be considered that they helped to give *Kimono My House* a commercial edge that may have not otherwise been there. That's not to say that Ron and Russell didn't have commercial potential anyway but certainly, the sound on *Kimono My House* was very much a group effort overall. Martin Gordon had a background in classical music and had been part of the National Jazz Youth Orchestra. As a result, he was able to contribute effectively on the arrangements when it came to making *Kimono My House.*

Kimono My House was recorded at the Who's Ramport Studio in south London. The studio time wasn't on the expensive side of things and furthermore, rehearsals that had taken place previously ensured that by the time they started recording, they sounded very much together already. However, Britain's 1974 power strikes had an effect on the recording schedule of *Kimono My House*, at least to an extent. Russell was quoted in *The Scotsman* in September 2005: "They told us that we could work from, like, noon to four – but after that there was no power. And then they said, 'Well lads, even if the record does get finished, there may not be enough vinyl to go around.' That wasn't part of our dream of conquering Britain."

So was the grass actually greener in Britain? Possibly not. Russell was quoted in *Record Collector* in July 2003: "'Tattoo' by the Who – we used to listen to that and think, we want to be as cool as that. 'Waterloo Sunset' (by the Kinks) – not only did we like it musically, but it was speaking of this utopian England. We came over and went to Waterloo

Bridge and Waterloo Station. It's not quite as romantic as it is on the record." I would imagine that Britain would be quite a strange place to visit for the first time, especially considering where the Mael brothers grew up and the extent of fantasy imagery they associated with Britain before they arrived.

A number of accounts stipulate that there were limits to the band's rapport and chemistry, both personally and professionally. The music perhaps doesn't show it but certainly, there are probably strong reasons as to why the project perhaps felt like "the Mael brothers and their band". Throughout their career, Ron and Russell have always been the front men of Sparks. It was presented as such to audiences when the band first did *Top Of The Pops* but also, in the studio, it comes across that Ron and Russell were very much at the forefront when it came to the ideas. It doesn't necessarily come down to an inability on their part to work well as part of a team though. The fact is that from an early age, the Mael brothers have shared a creative rapport, and in some ways, they're in their own world; really, there is some extent of inevitability to the band dynamics that may have been present during the making of *Kimono My House*. With Ron and Russell, rightly or wrongly, as the front men of Sparks, by the time *Kimono My House* had made its impact commercially, the brothers were in a position of being able to choose who would be in the band from that point onwards.

Musically, *Kimono My House* was representative of a change in sound that focussed on Ron's songwriting. Unlike the Bearsville days, by the time Sparks were on Island, it was officially the case that Ron was in the driving seat from a songwriting perspective. Tracks on the Bearsville albums that particularly highlight Sparks' older sound are covers of the Roger and Hammerstein songs, 'Do Re Mi' and 'Here Comes Bob' (which included a string section) as well as 'The Louvre' which contained both English and French lyrics (that said, Sparks had a strong French following by late 1974 so to have a song in their discography that gave a nod to the French might not have been such a bad thing).

Martin Gordon considered that Muff Winwood's strength as a producer was in how he looked at what the album needed as a whole, rather than getting bogged down in the finer details of it to an obsessively intricate extent. Equally, John Hewlett contributed very much as manager and not from a musical perspective.

During the sessions for *Kimono My House*, a song called 'Too Hot To Handle' kept cropping up. Written by Ron on the piano at his parent's house, it was dramatic, and apparently so because it was born out of Ron's frustration at not being able to get the hang of some Bach etudes. The aggressive sound of the piece was such that when lyrics were added, it lent itself to something that had themes of gunfighters having a showdown at sunset. The theme of the song was such that it strongly lent itself to having a wild west feeling to it. It was engineer Richard Digby Smith's idea to add gunshot sound effects to it. This was taken from a BBC *Sound Effects* record. When Digby Smith suggested the idea and played it to the band, a unanimous decision was made that it was right for the song. This is the song that eventually came to be called, 'This Town Ain't Big Enough For Both Of Us'. Ron wrote the song with such enthusiasm that it wasn't until he had finished doing so that it came to light that it wasn't in the ideal key to suit Russell's singing.

The vocal sound on 'This Town Ain't Big Enough For Both Of Us' was criticised by some under the consideration that it was "stylised". It is possible that some may have thought of the song in such regard due to the fact that it was written without Russell's vocal range in mind. Ron was quoted in *The Word* in February 2006: "'This Town Ain't Big Enough For Both Of Us' was written in A, and by God it'll be sung in A. I just feel that if you're coming up with most of the music, then you have an idea where it's going to go. And no singer is gonna get in my way."

To which Russell was quoted: "When he wrote 'This Town Ain't Big Enough For Both Of Us', Ron could only play it in that key. It was so much work to transpose the song and one of us had to budge, so I made the adjustment to fit in. My voice ain't a 'rock' voice. It's not soulful, in the traditional rock way; It's not about 'guts'. It's untrained, unschooled, I never questioned why I was singing high. It just happened, dictated by the songs. Ron has always written Sparks' lyrics and never transposed them into a rock key for me to sing. He always packed each line with words and I had to sing them as they were."

That's fascinating! So basically had Ron been the one willing the budge on the matter, Russell's vocals on 'This Town Ain't Big Enough For Both Of Us' would probably sound quite different, as in he might not have had to work as hard had he been able to negotiate for the song being in a different key.

When asked if he had ever had singing lessons, Russell was quoted in *The Guardian* in August 2017: "No, I never have. I've just had good luck." It's a unique voice and a very listenable one. If every single person who has gone without singing lessons could sing like Russell, then the world would have even more beautiful music in it.

Honestly, there are times when, live, Russell's voice has sounded a bit strained, even in the early days. There may have been value in taking vocal lessons in that regard

– if only for the purposes of studying techniques to get the best out of his voice from an ergonomic perspective. Really though, he sounds great and has stage presence so there is certainly nothing to complain about. I trust there are trained singers who couldn't deliver to such standard. Russell was quoted in *Sounds* in January 1975: "A lot of people I like were the West Coast groups like Jan and Dean and The Beach Boys. They had style but they weren't the traditional singer who went to vocal school. They sounded really youthful – a certain teen type singing that was a kid on the street who got up there and started singing."

Upon being asked which Sparks songs are the most difficult to sing, in *The Guardian* article Russell was also quoted as saying: "The difficult songs fall into two categories – the ones that have an insane amount of lyrics in them, and the ones that have the insane amount of range of the notes, going from incredibly high to low. Actually thinking about it, there are ones with an insane amount of lyrics and an insane range of notes – ones like 'At Home, At Work, At Play', even a song like 'This Town', the range of that song, and hitting that last F-sharp, the word 'leave', I have to psych myself up for the final note."

Ron was quoted of his brief stint with piano lessons in *Sounds* in December 1974; "I first took lessons when I was five. The thing that persuaded me was *big* parents – giving their son a little culture, spelt with a capital C. I really detested it pretty much at the time because I was really interested in sports and then I took it up again much later on. I got interested in rock music, I didn't see how it related to piano though. Little did I know that seventy-four short years later..." (Yep, Ron really did state that as a time frame!). When asked if he had any interest in singing, Ron was quoted in the same feature: "Not especially, 'cos, y'know, I have a really poor voice. I would like to maybe do a recording of some singing just for a giggle. It's definitely no ambition of mine."

David Betteridge popped into the studio every now and again to see how things were going but really, he was happy to leave things to Muff Winwood. He trusted that Winwood was right for the job because he had an understanding of the process from both a musician's perspective and a managerial one. Chris Blackwell kept to himself during the making of *Kimono My House*. Martin Gordon considered that it may have been down to Blackwell not being keen on Sparks, or at least seeing them commercially as a risk in the context of Island's existing portfolio at the time.

Having Muff Winwood as producer was probably very welcome indeed. With regards to the fact that Todd Rundgren did the production on Sparks' very first album on Bearsville, Ron was quoted in *Sounds* in June 1974: "It was a problem just because Todd was an artist as well as a producer and there's always a bit of conflict in interest in a way. We were very pushy for what we wanted on the first track. 'High C' – Todd was into harmonies and we were less into harmonies. Just from the start there were small things like that. We really liked Todd, but on a producer artist level it got to be a bit of a bind."

In the same feature, Ron was quoted of Muff Winwood's production on *Kimono My House:* "It's approaching the point of sounding like a traditional record. We sort of resigned ourselves to the fact that it wouldn't sound like a traditional recording which is what we set out to do. Muff's an amazing person to work with because once you get tired of the recording session you can listen to him speak with his Birmingham accent."

In total, it took sessions at a number of studios to

complete the recording of *Kimono My House:* Ramport, AIR, Wessex and Island's Basing Street studio. The album's title was decided upon at some point during the recording process. It is a pun on 'Come On-A My House' by Rosemary Clooney. The Mael brothers claim to have never spoken to Clooney.

It was towards the end of the recording of *Kimono My House* that the wheels were in motion for replacing Martin Gordon with Ian Hampton. John Hewlett already managed Ian Hampton when he was in Jook so there was scope for such crossover already in place. Martin Gordon was quoted in *Mojo* in August 2003: "(in May 1974) I had two shots at *Top Of The Pops* with Sparks. The first time we turned up, the manager hadn't arranged work permits for the two Californians, so the BBC asked us to go away. The next week we did 'This Town Ain't Big Enough For Both Of Us', and the week after that, I was out. I remember watching the *Top Of The Pops* performance go out on the Thursday after we'd recorded it. I'd just turned twenty and I was basking in the glow of minor celebrity. I went home to Hitchin on the Friday to celebrate with my pals, I got very drunk. At 4am the phone rang. It was a minion from Sparks' office. In a strained voice he said 'Hello Martin, how are you? By the way, they don't want you in the group anymore.' I remember the walls spinning but whether it was the alcohol or the news I'm not sure. But a couple of days later I signed away all my royalties for *Kimono My House* in perpetuity. I recently got my first income from the album, a cheque for £23. When John Hewlett was interviewed in the early nineties, he was asked why I was sacked. He said the Maels were intimidated by me, felt their creative control was threatened and that he was immature as a manager, he should have told them to behave themselves. I met him later in the nineties, he'd become a born-again Christian and told me he was very sorry about what had happened and that he'd pray for me. So that's alright then."

A quick and important note from me here, readers: I have quoted Martin Gordon because that is his side of the story and it is therefore relevant because he played on *Kimono My House* and he was part of Sparks' first appearance on *Top Of The Pops*. Gordon is an important part of Sparks' history. I have quoted him for that reason and that reason alone; his complaints about (and perspectives on) Sparks and Hewlett are his and his alone.

As soon as *Kimono My House* was finished, Hewlett was stringent in ensuring that the band were well rehearsed for live performances. With much confidence in Sparks, Hewlett booked time in the cinema on Fulham Road. It had been turned into what came to be known as Manticore Studios by Emerson, Lake and Palmer and was owned in partnership with Chris Blackwell. The acoustics in the cinema were such that it prompted an advert to be placed in *Melody Maker* for an organist.

This is where Peter Oxendale briefly comes into the story. In many resources relating to Sparks, Peter Oxendale is referred to as Sir Peter Oxendale. He was dubbed as such by Adrian Fisher. Essentially, it was banter that became immortalised.

Although Oxendale's time in Sparks was brief, he did go on to have success working with Chris de Burgh for a number of years. As well playing keyboards on Ian Hunter's *Overnight Angels* album in 1977, Oxendale played keyboards with Dead Or Alive and Frankie Goes To Hollywood.

Using the space and taking advantage of the good acoustics in Manticore, Sparks rehearsed for a week or so with Oxendale welcomed into the line-up. It was apparently during this time that tensions between the Mael brothers and Martin Gordon were reaching an intolerable height. Ron was quoted of Sir Peter Oxendale in *Sounds* in June 1974: "He was never in the band, we really had to have some meat in the bottom so we employed Peter to play at the live gigs."

'This Town Ain't Big Enough For Both Of Us' was given its first airing on 11th March 1974 on Capital Radio. It was on the 22nd that it was released as a single. John Peel held the single in high regard and succeeded to promote it as such on his Radio One show. He had already done this with some of Sparks' material that was released on Bearsville. Having John Peel on side has often been cited as something that has helped a number of artists come to prominence over the years. I think it's worth mentioning though that whilst Peel was championing Sparks as far back as their Bearsville days, it wasn't until Sparks changed musically that they were able to go the distance commercially. Besides, after its release, 'This Town Ain't Big Enough For Both Of Us' was a slow burner, in that it wasn't until the May that it really started to make an impact in the charts. However, in terms of the medium of radio overall, it probably had a lot more clout as a promotional tool in the UK than in the US.

In an interview with *Get Ready To Rock* in December 2007, Russell was quoted as he considered the differences between radio broadcasting in Europe and radio broadcasting in America, and how this may have been a factor in Sparks having more initial success in the former: "Things are transmitted around Europe in a more centralised kind of way and things get disseminated in Europe much easier. In America it's more fragmented, there's no centralised radio to cover the whole country so it has different things."

Sparks should have made their appearance on *Top Of The Pops* on 2nd May 1974 but proceedings got delayed due to the technical problem of the Mael brothers' work permit not having been organised in time. It is considered by some that Sparks being unable to perform on *Top Of The Pops* when they first turned up to do so harmed the chart position of 'This Town' and robbed the band of the opportunity to get the single to the number one spot. In Sparks' place, The Rubettes performed 'Sugar Baby Love' and it rocketed from number fifty-one to number one, where it remained for four weeks.

It's a good thing for Sparks that they were on *Top Of The Pops* in May. By June 1974, no episodes of the programme were made due to the BBC technician's strike. It continued into the month of August!

By the time the Mael brothers were on *Top Of The Pops*, they had been honing their craft as musicians and indeed performers for years up to that point. This was their moment. A video was actually made to accompany 'This Town Ain't Big Enough For Both Of Us'. It was directed by Rosie Samwell-Smith who was then wife to Paul Samwell-Smith of Yardbirds fame. The location for the shoot was at Lord Montague's Car Museum in the New Forest. Sadly perhaps, the video was barely shown. It was purely down to the fact that at the time, Britain only had three TV channels, where music programmes weren't shown frequently enough to carry music videos at the time. As a result, it was Sparks' performance of the song on *Top Of The Pops* that came to be the iconic and well known version.

Regarding the video, Russell was quoted in *Get Ready To Rock* in December 2007: "Yeah, well actually the 'This Town' video wasn't even a video it was a film as at that time there were no outlets to show that kind of thing. This was pre video days and there were no video channels or MTV. But Island Records positively encouraged us to come up with something and I think they wanted to capture the idea of the song on film in non concert kind of setting."

Besides, going on *Top Of The Pops* was a useful vehicle for Sparks in terms of how the medium of TV enhanced the scope for them to get the theatrical elements of their performance style across. Ron was quoted in *The Word* in February 2006: "Television had just become important and the close-up had begun to matter. On TV you could make an impact with a small, subtle action that would have had no effect in concert, in a big hall. You could strike people in a big way – a raised eyebrow, a changed expression, a moustache. I'd done them live before, but nobody had noticed! Now they began to have a massive effect."

During the seventies, going on *Top Of The Pops* was something of a double edged sword for some bands. On the one hand, it was an excellent means of getting an immediate extent of exposure to the record buying public but on the other hand, there was a risk of being seen as too mainstream and manufactured. Such dilemma always came with the risk that it would alienate some audiences. Ron was quoted in *Record Collector* in July 2003: "The level of notoriety was something. All of a sudden you've gone from playing to six people at the Whisky to being on *Top Of The Pops*, where twenty five per cent of the country saw you. The only downside was that the teenybop following alienated a section of those people who only wanted us to be an art-rock band. All of that screaming forced away a lot of the people who appreciated us musically." Overall, regardless of the demographic that accounted for Sparks' audience, the fact is that Sparks had their attention.

Ron was quoted in *Sounds* in June 1974: "There's always a problem for a band that doesn't know what it's doing, which is still the case with us, where people on the outside don't know what we're doing." Even with commercial success, there was possibly a sense that Sparks were still finding their feet overall.

With the single doing well and *Kimono My House* due for release, Hewlett began the search for assistance in the management department. Things were looking up in a big way and it was a job for someone who could hit the ground running. Larry Dupont didn't want the job and so who better to ask than a devoted fan who was both familiar with and passionate about Sparks' material. Enter one Joseph Fleury, the man behind Sparks' fan club. Lee Packham also came aboard, a natural choice seeing that he was Muff Winwood's PA at Island. The sales team comprised Island employees, Dave Domleo and Fred Cantrell.

Kimono My House was reviewed in *Beat Instrumental* in August 1974: "Perhaps the most important requirement for 'making it' is individuality. Sparks' music is different, although not so different as to be violently original. The most noticeable ingredient is Russell Mael's voice which combines with the staccato line music he writes (along with twin brother Ron who plays keyboards), to produce a jumpy, nervous kind of sound. The thing I like least about Sparks is the marketed image. Russell looks suitably pretty and he's offered frontline contrast by brother Ron who seems to have sought to find an image suitable to his dated Christian name, and opted for a Chaplinesque (sic) appearance. I suppose the band (and their management and record company) found it necessary for getting the *Top Of The Pops* slot that broke the record, but I hope they would drop the front fairly soon. Quite honestly this album shows them to be an extremely competent band who, in seeking an unusual sound, have found a song pattern that is instantly identifiable as theirs (a most important point).

The song of this album that really epitomises the peculiar melodic and rhythmic structures of the band is 'Equator' on side two. If you haven't already looked into this album, do so."

The sound at the end of 'Equator' is not too different to that of a saxophone. However, it is actually a sound that Ron was able to make on the keyboard (with added effects, of course). The whispering sound on the track is Russell's voice, but sped up. Oh, and Ron and Russell aren't twins. Ron is three years older than Russell and this is still the case today! Still though, it's fascinating to think that some people thought they were (non identical!) twins. It's understandable in terms of how the duo clearly had such a good working relationship as musicians.

Beginning their career in a Britain where they were relatively unknown, Sparks had the scope to play on the enigma surrounding their image. In a world where the media was not as prominent and there was no internet or social media, an enigma was much easier to maintain. Notably, the cover art on *Kimono My House* features two women in kimonos. They were both members of a Japanese dance company that was touring in England in 1974. The band, their name and the title of the album don't feature on the front cover. Still though, it is certainly a fun album cover, so much so that photos from the same shoot were included in Sparks' 1974 US press pack. One such photo includes the models laughing while one of them shows their middle finger to the camera.

The garish application of the cover models' makeup is such that some people thought they were men in drag. So much so that Russell was keen to clear this up in a number of interviews. In actual fact, the photoshoot took around four or five hours and there was an element of trial and error purely on account of the fact that no hair and makeup artists had been hired to work on the models. The two women weren't too sure on how to fix their kimonos either. That said, they were given freedom in terms of how they posed for the photographs. The one that was chosen as the image for the album cover was actually originally an outtake. The model on the right (with the fan), Michi Hirota, her husband – Joji Hirota – was the musical director of the Japanese dance company, Red Buddha Theatre. Island approached the managing director of the theatre company in search of Japanese women to model for Sparks' album cover. The name of the woman on the left of the album's cover is Kuniko Okamura.

Using his skills as a designer, Ron had already made a mock up of the album cover before it was shot. It featured two geishas looking at Sparks' previous album, A *Woofer In Tweeter's Clothing*, with disgust. Such a design concept certainly implies that Sparks had a sense of humour about where they had come from and, more importantly perhaps, where they were going. For the actual photoshoot for *Kimono My House*, Karl Stoecker did the photography. He was already known for his work on albums by Roxy Music.

In June 1974, a *Melody Maker* journalist mused on the universal popularity of Sparks:

> "Hey," the shopgirls would giggle, clustering together like iron filings drawn to a magnet, "it's them." And if the store had a record department someone would put on 'This Town Ain't Big Enough For Both Of Us', and then the girls' courage would grow with their numerical strength and Ron and Russell Mael would be pursued out of the shop.

And "Oh you lovely man," a middle aged woman at a soccer team social would say throwing her arms round a startled shoulder, "you must come over with us to our table." And Ron would be swept away by this vision with blonde hair piled on her head and lacquered wood-hard.

The over-forties love him and touch his 'tache to see if it's real. And after a gig, guys about twenty years old would bluster on to the group coach and demand, "Hey swap us yer tie. It's a Take Six, this one."

"Oh," Ron would answer politely, clearly not quite sure what was going on. And after a halting pause in which his face bore not a trace of the various emotions passing through his mind — confusion, embarrassment, flattery and the desire to neither swap his tie or offend his fan. "Oh, mine's a Marks and Spencer's. They're much better." So he takes the guy's address and promises to send him one.

Russell was quoted in *The Scotsman* in September 2005: "They'd run on stage and try to grab you, although if they got hold of you, they weren't quite sure what to do next."

Lost and damaged clothing was probably a standard occupational hazard for Sparks during their first tour of Britain in 1974. Joseph Fleury was tasked with popping out to buy more clothes for Russell after his outfit had been ruined by enthusiastic fans in Leeds. Muff Winwood was quoted in *Sounds* in July 1974: "Apparently a few girls grabbed Russ' trouser legs and began pulling him off the stage. Some roadies grabbed hold of him and he was suspended in mid air for a few minutes. In the end one of his trouser legs was ripped off."

Russell was quoted regarding how he felt about the hysterical reaction he had received from fans in *Sounds* in September 1974: "I enjoyed it. The only other approach we might take as opposed to having me out front is to have, that's if we decide to get another person, is possibly have a third person who is as strong. A sort of personality so there can be more conflict on stage. To add a third person makes it more aggressive visually."

It's fascinating to think that a third permanent Spark could have been invited to join the Mael's double act. Now though, with hindsight, considering the strong professional rapport between Ron and Russell that has lasted over four decades, it doesn't sound like it would have worked really. When asked how they got on as brothers, Ron was quoted in *Beat Instrumental* in August 1974: "Well, we're so much at odds anyway that we really don't have that many conflicts, we haven't got many similarities as part of the band."

Russell was quoted: "I'm thinking of kicking him out of the band because I'm getting pretty good on keyboards." Ron: "I'm going to quit anyway. No, the real things that bother us are who uses all the hot water or who gets to take the first bath, things like that." It was reported in *Melody Maker* in June 1974: "Together, they're never apart, have you noticed that, I'm asked? The only time they're ever apart is when they buy food for sandwiches. Ron goes to get the cheese while Russell goes to the bakery. Or is it the other way around? For brothers, they sure get on well. It's funny, says Muff, how he always works with brothers. First there was his own kid brother Stevie in the Spencer Davis Group. Then there was Iain and Gavin Sutherland. Now there's Ron and Russell."

Left to right: Adrian Fisher, Ron Mael, Dinky Diamond, Russell Mael and Martin Gordon.

Ron was quoted in *The Quietus* in August 2017: "It's always awkward for us working with other people (including the early days with ex Jook musicians) just because we work so much by ourselves. We don't worry about what the other person thinks in Sparks, but working with other musicians, you're always thinking, 'Are they gonna think this is lame?' Even though we've done this for so long, there's still a lot of insecurity in your abilities."

I advocate that this is a real eye opener; it would be so easy to look at the changing line-ups of Sparks throughout 1974 and wonder if the Mael brothers adopted a brutal strategy of hiring and firing musicians as part of seeing them as secondary team members. Really though, when taking into account that the creative rapport between Ron and Russell was so intense and has been for decades now, it's probably just one of those things in terms of, the rapport they have isn't something that could easily be shared with other musicians.

Chapter Four

Rising Stars

The scale of Sparks' fame in 1974 must have been challenging for the band at times. Russell was quoted in *Beat Instrumental* in August 1974: "I just went to buy some shampoo, and I just couldn't get it because there was a real scene in Woolworths. We enjoy being popular, but we still need to get shampoo and things, so it can be a real pain in the neck."

When asked if fame was all it's cracked up to be, Ron was quoted in the same feature: "Oh, it's better. The only thing that's strange is that you're not really aware of it happening. You see the charts and you see the record listed, and you can't, or aren't aware that that's you, you know. You see it as another band with the name Sparks. We enjoy it in a certain kind of way. If you knew somebody in another band and they began to achieve success you'd probably feel a lot better for them than it is for you."

That sounds incredibly surreal! When it was suggested by the interviewer that perhaps they couldn't really believe it was all happening, Russell was quoted: "Oh, you can believe it, but then it becomes that having the number two record isn't that significant because when somebody else has it, you go, 'so what's that?'"

Their original sound and image determined how Sparks were seen by UK audiences. There was an enigma about the band in terms of the Mael brothers image as well as in the fact that the rest of the band weren't in the spotlight (this was literally the case in terms of the live shows!). It was advocated in *Melody Maker* in June 1974:

> It would be easy to dismiss the four Anglos in Sparks as "extras" in the Mael stage show. The lights, for instance, concentrate almost exclusively on Ron and Russell Mael so that for the major part of the seventy-five-minute set guitarists Adrian Fisher and Trevor White and bassist Ian Hampton are in shadow. Drummer Dinky Diamond is in the spotlight only because Russell stands immediately in front of Dinky's drum pedestal and the spot that picks out the Mael shines on the Diamond too.

> But it isn't Mael plus backup. A lot of trouble went into finding the right balance in Sparks. Trevor and Ian joined from Jook only recently after Martin Gordon, who played bass on *Kimono My House*, was unwilling to do what was required. And Sir Peter Oxendale, who was going to be an unseen organist in the wings, was similarly not cut out to be a Spark.

> So White took over as second guitarist and they have a harder, edgier sound because, as it happens, the organ on the album doesn't play too important a role yet many of the guitar parts were overdubbed and four hands are better than two.

The Mael brothers may have seen things differently though. It may not have been their intention to present Sparks as being themselves plus a backup band. Ron was quoted in *Sounds* in June 1974: "Sparks isn't just backup musicians for the two of us. It's a real band and so the things that are really traditional in a way about rock, about bands and about the rock ritual of playing live in front of a live audience, those are things that I think are really strong and I really like playing live. You can't always get the idea from a record because a record is always detached from everything and you can't get things into that kind of perspective."

It was reported in *Melody Maker* in July 1974:

The story of Sparks has two main characters. Ron and Russell Mael from California. The British contingent isn't so well known. After two albums in the States as Halfnelson and then as Sparks, the Maels with Jim and Earle Mankey and Harley Feinstein came to Britain when their single, 'Wonder girl', threatened to become a hit in the States.

After barely half a dozen gigs in several months, they went back to the States, quit their label, Bearsville, and split up. The Maels thought about an early retirement but first called Hewlett, who'd helped them through their English visit. He encouraged them, got them over to England, Muff Winwood signed them to Island Records.

They formed a band with Dinky Diamond on drums, guitarist Adrian Fisher, and bassist Martin Gordon. Their single, 'This Town Ain't Big Enough

For Both Of Us', became a big hit. So did their
Kimono My House album. A tour was already set
up and organist Sir Peter Oxendale was employed
to play offstage. He was never a permanent
member of the band.

Before the tour, Oxendale and Gordon were
fired and Trevor White (second guitar) and Ian
Hampton (bass) were brought in from Jook,
another of Hewlett's brainchild bands.

Russell was quoted in *Sounds* in June 1974: "We
decided, before we started playing, to have the strongest
line-up that we could get."

Joseph Fleury was quoted in *Sounds* in July 1974: "The
visual aspect of the band has improved immensely since
the change of line-up. Russell used to run up and down the
stage and it got hectic at times but now he's developing an
act. Ron has always been the same. He cut his moustache
after the first album. But his hair used to be like Russ' and
they used to look identical. I think now he's cut his hair, the
brothers come out as two individual characters."

Some of the media probably didn't quite know how to
take Sparks, the Mael brothers and their brand of music.
Was it a constructed image? Were they being weird and
eccentric for its own sake? Ron was quoted in the Texas
paper, *The Marshall News Messenger*, in July 1975: "I was
bored with looking at bands where everyone looked the
same. I never felt comfortable with long hair so it didn't
make sense to be looking that way."

When asked who thought up Sparks' image, Ron was
quoted in *Beat Instrumental* in August 1974: "I don't even
see it especially as an image even. The connotation I have
of an image is where you actually sit down in a health food

restaurant and work it out. It wasn't that way. It was just sort of doing it and finding something that was us."

In response to the interviewer asking how long his hair used to be, Ron was quoted: "When I first came to England it was long. It was at the point where, for me, I could see that being a rock and roll type of person wasn't right... From the people close to us, no one really liked the haircut."

Russell was quoted: "We went into a hair place one day and I had an inch off and he went in and he said cut it really short and that's how he came out." When asked about his image as the "non-smiling, not participating keyboard player", Ron was quoted in the same feature: "Oh, I've always been like that. I'd look like a real idiot if I leapt about."

Really though, that in itself is a performance. In the same feature, Russell stated that they had five years' experience of being on stage at that point. Really, the Mael brothers had had a taste of being in the spotlight – at least to some extent – from a young age. With regards to their formative years modelling clothes in a mail-order catalogue, Russell was quoted in *The Irish News* in June 2018: "The photos might be in a box in the attic somewhere, but hopefully nobody will be seeing those!" Russell was quoted in *Record Collector* in July 2003: "It wasn't really child acting. We did some catalogue modelling things. It was more standing in front of a camera and smiling than Shakespeare... It wasn't the basis of anything that prepared us for anything."

It was advocated of the Mael brothers in *New Musical Express* in November 1974: "The interesting thing about Ron and Russell in the flesh is their staggering normalcy, though maybe that makes them weird. They're the original clean livers – honey, orange juice, compote de fruit and calisthenics – no smoking or alcohol – keeps them young and fit. Both of them too have highly developed savoir-fair and cultivated charm which guides them through the trickiest situations with dignity. At one point, Russell is accosted by an elderly (hotel) guest who mistook him for the waiter ('coffee please young man'). Without the least hesitation, he obliges. Perfect service. But then that, of course, is what Sparks are all about."

From the perspective of UK audiences, it is understandable as to how Sparks could have been regarded as, for better or for worse, an overnight success. In a number of interviews, the brothers were keen to assert that really, they had been working at their craft for quite a bit longer.

Ron was quoted in *New Musical Express* in November 1974: "At first, they said we'd made it too soon, but of course, we'd been without success for five years." It was reported in the same feature: "Recalling early gigs at the Whisky in LA, where the original band started, has Russell bemoaning English weather and reminiscing nostalgically over old stage surprises. Apparently Russell used to wield a sledge hammer during '(No More) Mr Nice Guys'. Just for fun, you understand, but on one memorable occasion he inadvertently let it slip and had to have twenty-five stitches in his head, although he finished the show with blood streaming from the wound. A more successful, less deadly effect was the boat pushed across the stage by a roadie for 'Showboat' from which he showered the audience, if there were any, with bouquets and candy. If you're looking for such embellishments this time around you'll be disappointed. Ian (Hampton) is adamant that the group are concentrating on musical presentation rather than visual sensation." Russell was quoted of their time at the Whisky A Go Go in *Record Collector* in July 2003: "It attracted Todd Rundgren, which was validation enough."

Kimono My House got to number four in the UK

albums chart and it was awarded gold status by the British Phonographic Industry in September 1974. Also, the 'This Town Ain't Big Enough For Both Of Us' single was certified silver in June 1974 (one of Sparks' earlier songs was 'Barbecutie'. It was being considered for release as the debut single in Britain. The track was however, used as the B-side on 'This Town Ain't Big Enough For Both Of Us'). Considering the release dates of both Sparks' debut album and debut single on Island, it was a seriously speedy success.

Later in the summer, the 'Amateur Hour' single also got to number seven in the UK and number twelve in Germany. It was advocated in the *Coventry Evening Telegraph* on 24th July 1974: "It's a good week for singles too, with Sparks – who appear to be the 'in' band at the moment – leading the way with 'Amateur Hour', a typically frantic offering from their top selling *Kimono My House* album. Should be a top tenner." It certainly was!

The 'Amateur Hour' single was reviewed in *Sounds* in July 1974: "If I had to pick the most important 'new' band of 1974, I'd select either Sparks or Be-Bop Deluxe. Neither are new, of course, but you know what I mean. Ultimately, because they've had a greater impact on what one calls 'the scene', I'd go for Sparks. Close though, decided on penalties. Anyway, I saw 'em in action recently in Cambridge and it must be said that the sound wasn't too hot. The most impressive feature of their Island Records is the astonishing clarity that Muff Winwood conjured out of the studio air; that – and Sparks' highly individual stylings and lyrics. They're as bright and as brash as an expensive new sports car – but they have the added ingredient of it. In short (as I'm sure you know) superb. This single, an obvious choice, comes from their essential LP and I'm sure you already know it well. If you don't, then scurry down to your nearest record shop and learn every note of it. There'll be questions next week."

It was reported in *Melody Maker* in June 1974: "Cockney Rebel and Sparks — the two major new phenomena of British rock. They've both begun their first British tours and are both going down a storm!... Sparks, with their new Anglo-American line-up, climax their tour at London's Rainbow Theatre on Sunday July 7th. Their new single is out on July 12th. It features two new songs by pianist Ron Mael. Titles are 'Something For The Girl With Everything' and 'Lost And Found'. Reaction to their tour has been phenomenal. At Leeds, the third night, the show was delayed until the crowd was calmed but at least twenty girls were carried out of the hall once the band came on." (1974 was also a massive year for Cockney Rebel. In May 1974, *New Musical Express* reported that the band were due to start their first British tour. A highlight of the itinerary was to be a gig at London's Victoria Palace Theatre on 23rd June. In 1974, Cockney Rebel's album, *The Best Years Of Our Lives* was released. It was produced by the Beatles' recording engineer, Alan Parsons, and included the track 'Make Me Smile (Come Up And See Me)' which would go on to be a UK number one single in February 1975. It was at number one for two weeks and was the band's biggest selling hit. It sold over one million copies globally).

Sparks' gig at London's Rainbow was made possible by the fact that the option of performing at the London Palladium had been rejected. It's not clear regarding the who/how/why of the decision but it didn't seem to be to the detriment of the band. It was reported in *New Musical Express* in June 1974:

Dates and venues have now been finalised for a

fifteen-venue British concert tour by Sparks, plans for which were revealed by NME three weeks ago. But the band have now scrapped a project to appear at the London Palladium and will instead highlight their itinerary with a major concert at London's Rainbow, for which tickets go on sale this Saturday (15th).

Two newcomers have now become official members of the band – they are Tee White (Trevor White) (second guitar) and Ian Hampton (bass), and they join the existing nucleus of Ron and Russell Mael, Adrian Fisher and Dinky Diamond.

Sparks are currently in the Island studios with producer Muff Winwood recording three tracks, from which a new single will be selected for release on July 5th.

Meanwhile, Warner Brothers – for whom the original Sparks outfit recorded – are issuing a single called 'Girl From Germany' on June 18th. It is taken from an earlier album and is released, say Island, "to capitalise on the band's current popularity". Sparks will be supported in their Rainbow concert by G. T. Moore and the Reggae Guitars.

The *Acton Gazette* advocated of 'Girl From Germany' in July 1974: "Now that Sparks have really made their mark, here is a re-release of one of their older numbers taken from the *Woofer In Tweeter's Clothing* album. This time, the vocals sound more like Marc Bolan (whatever happened to him by the way?) and the rhythm is kept going by a battery of acoustic guitars. It's a pleasant enough tune, but it wouldn't stand much chance of being a hit if it wasn't riding in the wake of 'This Town Ain't Big Enough For Both Of Us'."

"Girl From Germany' was reviewed in *Melody Maker* in July 1974: "(I) can't imagine either Island or the Mael brothers being too pleased with the release of this track from the second Sparks album, *Woofer In Tweeter's Clothing*. Actually, it doesn't sound too bad, although it lacks the kind of manic urgency and vocal eccentricity which made the *Kimono My House* album such a killer. (There are) some nice touches in the chorus though, with some rather demented whistling behind Russell's distinctive falsetto. Could well prove more successful this time round."

Really, even if it was felt by Sparks that 'Girl From Germany' wasn't their best work (and I'm not saying that such was the case by any means), releasing some of their older material to capitalise on the success of 1974 probably wasn't such a bad idea at the time. The record buying public certainly had an enthusiasm for Sparks by that point.

In the readers' questions section of *Melody Maker* in April 1974, one reader asked "Are they still together, any news on an English tour, have they a fan club and what is their latest record?" to which the answer was given:

Yes, Sparks are still together. They began as an American band recording for Bearsville, and when this broke up, the two leaders, Ron and Russell Mael, reformed with a British rhythm section. They signed with Island and began recording their first album with Muff Winwood producing. This is about to be issued and is titled *Kimono My House*.

They also have a single on Island titled 'This Town Ain't Big Enough For Both Of Us' which comes from the LP.

Their names and instruments are Ron Mael: RMI electric piano with Echoplex reverb unit, two H/H 100 watt amps, two H/H 4 x 12 cabinets, Fender Twin Reverb unit as a monitor. Russell Mael: vocalist, who uses the RSE PA system, which is rented from Livewire and the size is varied to suit each venue. Sir Peter Oxendale: Hammond C3 organ, two Leslie speakers, two H/H 4 x 12 cabinets. Martin Gordon: Blonde Rickenbacker stereo bass guitar, two H/H 100 watt amps, four 4 x 12 H/H cabinets. Adrian Fisher: Black Gibson Les Paul, Marshall 100 watt amp, two Marshall 4 x 12 cabinets, various pedal attachments for guitar. Dinky Diamond: Premier drum kit with 22 inch bass drum and Avedis Zildjian cymbals.

No news so far about a British tour.

Their fan club is run by Joseph Fleury.

The fact that no tour dates were known in April is suggestive that the British tour was planned very quickly. The information about equipment is more detailed than many people might prefer or indeed understand but still, I've transcribed it because I trust it will be of value to some. It was reported in *Melody Maker* in June 1974:

Sparks are finally on the road and loving every minute of it. Last Thursday night, a little after 11pm, the band got on stage at the Cleethorpes Winter Gardens, an unglamorous enough opening date recalling memories of the previous all-American Sparks who used to play at the weirdest of places.

The new Anglo-American Sparks are playing what they had hoped was an "out of the way" gig to pull their act together. But once they'd advertised the dates it was obvious that many people from London were hot footing it up to Humberside.

So why advertise the gigs? Well, the first half dozen or so weren't going to be but, says Muff Winwood, the band's record producer, the rehearsals sounded so good that they had no fears about how the band would perform. Thus, the ads. And the guests, the fans and the curious descend on Cleethorpes. Last week," says a young bouncer at the Winter Gardens, which is as humid as a Turkish Baths, "we had Cockney Rebel in. Sparks outsold them by a hundred tonight, didja see the queues?"

So who comes to see Sparks? Walking from the front of the stage, pushing through the crush towards the back of the hall was like journeying through the seven ages of man. The youngest of young girls in front of the stage ready to scream and reach out for young Russell Mael and to stare bewildered and smile nervously at awe inspiring Ron Mael. Back through the crowd — the eighteen year olds in their big-night-out best, the twenty year olds in long hair and t-shirts, the twenty four years olds in Littlewoods chic, the twenty six year olds and then a final layer of thirty year old pluses.

Sparks are all things to all men, it seems, and the converted and the curious mingle in sweaty anticipation."

The feature continued:

Just about the time when the fishermen of Cleethorpes were getting restless, the lights went out. Sparks groped their way onto the stage. Dinky fell over his drum pedestal and a roadie let off a stink bomb. The heat from the lights (co-ordinated by Johnathan Sweeney, who did Hawkwind's light show) and from the bodies in the hall, pushed the stage temperature to around one hundred degrees.

Suddenly there is no longer time for nerves, which have never been fluttering from stomach to stomach like a butterfly from flower to flower (though it must be admitted that the manager John Hewlett and Muff Winwood seemed more nervous than any Spark). A delicate piano part opens and a spot picks out Ron. There is a God Almighty cheer. Folks just love Ron. There is a crashing guitar chord, a thudding, building, eight-to-the-bar drum pounding like an elephant charging up a flight of stairs. Russell's own spot picks him out and follows him as best it may. The guitars play with a thick, deep, luxurious tone. And Russell sings about trying to get laid in foreign parts which has two great lines ('You mentioned Kant and I was shocked/You know, where I come from none of the girls have such foul tongues') and calls to mind something the Maels said about liking the tourist experience where you get to see only the good side of the resort of town you're visiting.

Two and a half verses and two choruses into the first number,' Hasta Mañana Monsieur', Adrian flicks off a short sharp solo, Russell dances a tango and the song thunders. Then 'Talent Is An Asset' which has an opening melody line something like 'These Are A Few Of My Favourite Things' and is a fine song and, as with many other Sparks songs, the tune is often so torturous that the lyrics lose some of their impact. It's about a child genius and calls to mind the Maels in California who were lovers of music and baseball and arty things and football. And the coaches with their marine cropped hair were suspicious of "anything in which the word art was mentioned," says Russell, "You were immediately a little bit funny — somehow doing anything creative isn't masculine."

The artistic athletes or athletic artists on stage are already dripping with sweat. Ron's stone-like expression fleetingly bears the merest hint of a smile as he catches the eye of a girlie staring at him. Then he frowns and looks through eyes which seem unseeing at a spot far outside the seaside hall, several miles off-shore. Or he will offer a slight frown and a slight pursing of the lips and look down at his enormous hands which lightly clonk chords as he sits in the spotlight.

Still from the same feature:

Russell is all action in his white kimono style suit, which is rapidly drenched in sweat. And, Good God! It's shrinking. It's made of crepe and is reacting with starling speed to the perspiration. Already the sleeves have retreated halfway up the Mael forearm.

Russell sings with a hand on hip in high camp, with the left foot pawing at the stage floor like a Shetland pony stamps a hoof in a circus, with a hand wagging in mock lecture, with a skittering run across stage, with an impatient frantic look as though he had something to do in the next sixty seconds but couldn't for the life of him recall what or where it was.

They're playing 'In My Family' now, a racing bouncing song. Then, 'Thank God It's Not Christmas' starting with guitars on a descending run, notes rushing out like a man tumbling downstairs. Fisher and White are impressing, and as the song reaches the second chorus (after seven verses), Fisher takes another brief pointed solo. Another chorus, another solo then the stage eclipses into darkness as Ron is left alone touching the piano keys softly and sitting straight-backed in the glow of the only spotlight. There is a great roar. A magic moment that, they still love Ron ("That's the first time I've ever been applauded for a solo. Probably the first time anyone's been applauded for a one note solo ever," he said the next day).

A number from the old *Woofer* album, 'Girl From Germany' and then 'Barbecutie' (flip of 'This Town') and Russell's suit has all but shrunk to the size of a tea towel so he takes it off and puts on a jumper and the girls squeal at his pale skinny chest ("It wasn't", says Ron, "until the British Invasion that looking like a scarecrow was the desirable thing as opposed to looking like a lorry driver").

Russell does punches in the air and looks like a little lost kid while Ron hunches his shoulders and looks sinister, like a malevolent Dickens character. 'Here In Heaven', with its gut guitar and then the new single (out in July) called 'Something For The Girl With Everything'. It has sudden leaps into falsetto and would murder the less flexible throat (Russell: "It wasn't until we came to England that I started drinking hot tea and that seems to have helped my voice a lot." That's what's known as a PG Tip?).

Another unfamiliar number to most Anglo ears — 'Wonder girl', the hit US single which fades and with its dying note segues into Ron's piano intro to 'This Town' and there is a cheer much as you'd expect. Here too, the girls at the front start to press in. The crush had so far been well controlled by this hall's bouncers — and only one girl, even during 'This Town', had to be hauled away like a sack of potatoes. The crowd had parted like the Red Sea at Moses' command and she'd fallen as though pole-axed.

The cheer at the end of the number was enormous and they did 'I Like Girls' and 'Complaints' and the stage was again plunged into darkness and they groped their way off.

Sparks could have played an encore but they didn't, which in these days of gratuitous encores was pleasing to see. The show was over. The first night of a new band completed. Ron, his white accountant's shirt unbuttoned at the collar and his tie loosened, looked as "untidy" as anyone is ever likely to see him. Russell's clothes wrinkled and shrunk alarmingly. Trevor, who stands behind Ron and next to the stage left lights, will end the tour with a violent tan down his left side if those lights can bronze a person, Ian and Ade look suitably shattered. No one is nervous anymore and Dinky is as red as a lobster and looks close to collapse.

Just a few points to iron out. Russell's introductions are too long and destroy the fast-flow of the set. The lights need tightening up, especially the spots. When fans are more familiar with the album, the scenes will be shattering.

It was considered in the same feature:

Cleethorpes Winter Gardens was a strange place to open a tour but it'd been no weirder than the Maels playing at the Gaiety Delicatessen. Or at the Mormon Dance where no one was supposed to dance or have remotely suggestive lyrics sung to them. "Oh," the Mormons said to Russell, he recalls, "we actually didn't want a group that was danceable and that you could actually hear the beat."

"And we also got booked to open", says Ron, "this recreation centre around Watts, which is a black ghetto. It was, uh, a little odd because..."

"They thought", continues Russell, "we were soul music."

"Yeah, and the things we were playing then were well, really lightweight in the beat way. It was impossible to dance to excepting jigging or polking or something like that," says Ron.

"And one thing", concludes Russell, "that you don't want in Watts is a polka."

Then there was the time they played Max's Kansas City. *Melody Maker*'s Roy Hollingsworth saw them there in October 1972 and wrote, "Yes, I know who they remind me of – Dave Dee, Dozy, Beaky, Mick and Tich – and a poor version of them too – Sparks continued to play a brace of instantly forgettable tunes. It's a shame because they're good guys, but somebody should tell them that their cause is quite lost."

Well, it's nineteen months on now and their cause is quite won. They have a number two single which would have been number one if they had had the breaks with *Top Of The Pops* (they were due to go on just after the single came out but had work permit trouble and so The Rubettes got the spot and their single went to number one. That kept 'This Town' on the "bubblers" list for three weeks and by the time it got into the charts it had already sold a decent number of copies).

The album is also now selling like a good rock album should. Can you find a hole in their defences? They sell pop singles, rock albums and attract at least three generations of concert goers. The point is not being overstated. They are facts.

Sparks' first tour of Britain in 1974 was a well thought out operation. It had to be really; the band was well rehearsed and having quickly come to the attention of a British audience via their first appearance on *Top Of The Pops*, there was everything to play for in the live arena.

Still though, financially, things needed to be carefully balanced amongst the excitement of it all. It was reported in *Melody Maker* in June 1974:

The drive to the next gig in Hull helped explain why Sparks will be lucky to break even this tour. They're travelling in a forty-one seater coach. It is costing about £850 for the eighteen dates, and that doesn't include the driver's tabs. The lighting costs £100 a day, the PA runs at about £250 a day. In all, says manager Hewlett, the show is costing around £550 a day on the road.

The Hull gig was sold out in ninety minutes when the £1 tickets went on sale. Some of the tickets have been re-sold by students (the venue was the University of Hull) for £4 to kids in the town. The social secretary had booked Sparks well in advance of their single (it was in fact the first tour date confirmed).

Incredibly, the original bill for the night read "Cockney Rebel and The Rubettes supporting Sparks". Three top three recording acts, that would've been some battle of the bands huh? For some reason Cockney Rebel and The Rubettes pulled out. George Melly and a girl folk singer were added. It still looked like an intriguing night.

It was reported in the same feature:

The mood in Hull is a relaxing and encouraging one. A reporter in Holland phoned and said he'd heard already that the first night in Cleethorpes had been great and he was coming over later in the tour, was that okay?

"News travels fast doesn't it?" says an incredulous Hewitt.

The Rainbow gig is almost sold out in the first week. That will be an important show and the clear thinking behind these fairly remote provincial gigs becomes obvious but they're still getting letters saying, "Why no Manchester or Liverpool or Glasgow or Newcastle?"

There's a fuller tour planned in the autumn. At the Hull gig the band is better. Russell talks too much still, the lights aren't right yet (Ade plays a solo and should be hit with a spot but his head is missed and he looks like a phantom headless guitarist). Russell leans on the piano and he shakes the mic in his up-stretched hands as thought sprinkling pepper over the whole band. Ian on bass is missed by the spots when he starts 'Barbecutie'. The set is identical to the previous night. They get on their feet with 'This Town' and then it's straining hands and eager faces all over again. The guitars sound particularly strong, so punchy you find yourself involuntarily laughing. Mad.

Tonight there was no denying the encore. The ovation was no greater or smaller than in Cleethorpes yet it was more insistent and brooked no argument. We want more, it said, and we want it now. They got 'Amateur Hour', a song about puberty and growing up and learning the first bite of the apple. Like Ron's lyrics say, you can't start playing violin and sound like Y. Menuhin. Something like getting a tour together in the provinces before the biggie. These guys sure do practice what they preach.

A disco in a Hull hotel is receiving an unexpected preview of Sparks' next single, 'Something For The Girl With Everything'. The acetate was worn thin by morning. Drinks had been forced on Ron and Russell, who didn't imbibe and who sat there with Pernods until they left.

In July 1974, *Melody Maker* listed the equipment that Sparks were using on stage around that time:

Ian Hampton: Fender Jazz bass guitar. Two HH amps, two HH IC One hundreds, two Marshall 4 x 15 cabinets (200 watts).

Trevor White: Gibson Les Paul Custom and Guild S100 guitars. Marshall 100w stack.

Ade Fisher: Gibson Arrow and Gibson Les Paul Custom guitars, Marshall 100 watt cabinet.

Ron Mael: RMI electric piano with echoplex unit through Fender Twin Reverb amp (100 watt)

Dinky Diamond: Premier Custom drum kit comprising 26" x 17" bass drum, 15" x 10", 16" x 16" and 16" x 18" tom toms, 14" x 16" snare. Cymbals are 16", 18" and 20" Super Zyn, 14" Avedis and 15" matched Paiste hi hats. Dinky uses Foote C sticks and a Rogers bass drum pedal. All accessories are Premier.

PA is hired from Electrosound. It takes 2500 watts, uses 13 Shure mics and a 20 channel mixer.

Russell was quoted in *Beat Instrumental* in August 1974: "We use all our own gear but we hire a PA system... I don't know what PA we've hired. Ron's got an RMI electric piano and we use Marshall and HH amps." The brothers had certainly come a long way since their days of struggling to get a drumkit together. Ron was quoted in *Sounds* in June 1974: "I really like playing live because it puts you on the basis of being a regular band in a certain way, which is what we've really always wanted to be."

It was reported in *Sounds* in July 1974:

The crash began after the first half hour, just when Ron Mael led into 'This Town Ain't Big Enough For Both Of Us' with the familiar keyboard intro which brought the seated masses surging to the front of the stage. Two girls fainted and were hauled out of the crowd, but the rest continued to try and paw at Russell Mael as he cavorted about the stage. But the stewards — a true band of heavies — did a marvellous restraining job at Plymouth's one thousand seater mobile theatre.

Ironically, the giant theatre has been erected especially for a visit of the Royal Ballet later this month to the city.

Up to that point, Sparks had received a warm but restrained welcome, storming through a handful of early songs which were indecipherable thanks to the bad sound balance that swamped Russell's vocals in a cacophony of guitars and drums. Ron's keyboard thumping surfaced from time to time however, as he peered into the distance immaculate in collar and tie and neatly combed hair. 'Thank God It's Not Christmas' and 'Girl From Germany' were highlighted, although the obvious hurdle which Sparks will overcome with the passage of time, is the audience's unfamiliarity with the tunes.

It's easy to forget the rest of the band with the spotlight continually on the Mael brothers: guitarist Trevor White and Adrian Fisher and bassist Ian Hampton built a solid foundation for Russell's wide vocal range and drummer Dinky Diamond is a very forceful player who holds the whole thing together.

Sparks ended with an album track, 'Something For The Girl With Everything', then an encore, and that was it. Someone said it was a pity all their numbers sounded the same. They weren't in fact, but the volume blurred them beyond recognition. It could have been very good, but it was just too loud. Some bands need to find their lack of ability being a wall of noise. Sparks don't.

In July 1974, *Sounds* reported on Sparks' performance in Birmingham:

Cries of "we want Sparks" filtered their way into the back of the hall where the band were preparing themselves for the concert. Scene round the front — Something that I found rather pleasing was that instead of featuring a support act, there was a disco which was substantial enough to get the kids pepped up. The audience varied from the ages of fifteen to twenty, from the heads to the boppers, even the guys and gals that don't normally come to concerts, as opposed to the Cockney Rebel's gig which looked like a scene out of Shel Silverstein's *Freaker's Ball*. The reception to the band's entrance was thunderous, tumultuous — well bloody loud. The boys looked good. Russell in a casual dressing gown type jacket and trousers, Ronny in his infamous *Great Gatsby* look — hair greased back, white shirt and tie and baggy trousers, perched menacingly behind his Fender Rhodes electric piano. A quick "Hello" from Russ and the band went straight into 'Hasta Mañana Monsieur' and it was immediately noticeable that live, the music has become much harder and forceful to the point that the audience were stomping their feet in time. Ron's style of music forces an unusual amount of energy to be unleashed from the group, making them sweat and constantly move about — all apart from Ron, of course. He sits there perched over the piano, his Neanderthal type forehead and piercing glare staring at everything and nothing in particular. His features are stiff, almost statuesque, as opposed to Russ who marches up and down the stage like a clockwork soldier, his angelic features drawing screams from the girls in the front row...

The lighting and sound was on par, they've certainly taken in a choice road crew. Most of the

Sparks

THE CRASH began after the first half hour, just when Ron Mael led into "This Town Ain't Big Enough For The Both Of Us" with the familiar keyboard intro which brought the seated masses surging to the front of the stage.

Two girls fainted and were hauled out of the crowd, but the rest continued to try and paw at Russell Mael as he cavorted about the stage. But the Stewards — a true band of heavies — did a marvellous restraining job at Plymouth's 1,000 seater mobile theatre. Ironically, the giant theatre has been erected especially for a visit of the Royal Ballet later this month in the city.

Up to that point, Sparks had received a warm but restrained welcome, storming through a handful of early songs which were indecipherable thanks to bad sound balance that swamped Russell's vocals in a cacophony of guitars and drums. Ron's keyboard thumping surfaced from time to time however, as he peered into the distance, immaculate in collar and tie and neatly combed hair.

"Thank God It's Not Christmas" and "Girl From Germany" were highlighted, although the obvious hurdle which Sparks will overcome with passage of time, is the audience's unfamiliarity with the tunes.

It's easy to forget the rest of the band with the spotlight continually on the Mael brothers: guitarist Trevor White and Adriene Fisher and bassist Ian Hampton built a solid foundation for Russell's wide vocal range, and drummer Dinky Diamond is a very forceful player who holds the whole thing together.

Sparks ended with an album track, "Something For The Girls With Everything", then an encore, and that was it.

Someone said it was a pity all their numbers sounded the same. They weren't in fact, but the volume blurred them beyond recognition.

It could have been very good, but it was just too loud. Some bands need to find their lack of ability being a wall of noise — Sparks don't. — DAVID HARRIS

NEVER TURN YOUR BACK ON RUSS AND RONALD

No, it doesn't make you go blind. Russ Mael's been exciting himself for years now, in fact he owes his success to it

"You have to have a little blind faith in what you're doing . . . take a chance"

lights were aimed at Ron and Russ...

'Talent Is An Asset' followed, still with that
crazy marching beat and cram filled with lyrics.
Ron's style seems to be some kind of a musical
endurance test. I was quite dubious whether
Russell's vocals would have the same range as on
the album. Have no fear Sparklites, they're good.

The feature continued:

They went through most of their *Kimono* material.
'Here In Heaven' — "this one's about a pact", says
Russ in a childlike voice and wide eyed stare
(the girls love that), "that went wrong." Russell
teasingly walked across the front of the stage
and nearly got dragged into the crowd a couple
of times. The crowd roared with approval when
the band announced 'Girl From Germany', an old
number off their *A Woofer In Tweeter's Clothing*
(album) and it sounded fresher with their new
line-up. 'Wonder Girl' was the most subdued
number of the night... This goes straight into
'This Town' which was virtually drowned out
by cheering. "Now we're going to do a little
experiment with you, this track might be our
next single. It's really fast and really short," said
Russ and counted the band into 'Something
For The Girl With Everything', which I'll have
to hear a couple more times, but from what I
can make out of it, it sounds good. 'Thank God
It's Not Christmas' featured a three second solo
spot from Ron, who played some jumpy chords
and creased up into a devious smile. Adrian

did some particularly fine soloing, wielding his Flying Arrow guitar, occasionally leaping across the stage. Ian, who had been working hard all night, was beginning to look a bit tired, but he still managed to make his playing sound fresh and powerful. 'Complaints' had a nice jiving beat along with 'Barbecutie'. The audience knew every number and a lot of them were miming the lyrics. The encore was inevitable and the crowd screamed out for 'Amateur Hour' – their request was granted and the band finished the night off in great style.

Ron was quoted of the gig in the same feature: "The place wasn't full enough and there seemed to be something missing. It hasn't been the best night." Hmmm, perfectionism maybe? Or simply high aspirations? Either way, Ron's perception of the gig seemed to be held in lower regard to what the reporter made of it, who concluded the article: "There's no doubt that the band are going to be huge. They've managed to attract the boppers and the heads so their appeal is covering a huge market. Well it's about time something new happened innit? It might be unusual, eccentric, whatever, no matter what classification you put it under, it's good quality stuff. Love them or hate them, you'll still get a kick out of seeing them."

I've quoted from a number of gig reviews very generously there. But I make absolutely no apology for it. The amount of detail in the vintage articles shows the extent to which Britain was interested in Sparks in 1974 and the details included in such features need to be documented in the interest of preserving a phenomenal legacy really.

As far as bootlegs go, compared to many bands who

toured Britain at the time, there isn't an abundance of recordings available. In such regard, where vintage archiving might serve as a means of at least describing Sparks' live performances at the time then I'm all for it, as I know many others will be too. It was reported in *Melody Maker* in June 1974: "The towns get bigger. In Leeds on Saturday twenty girls fainted. In Cheltenham on Sunday Russell ended up on the floor of the stage having his trousers ripped off. Talent is their asset."

In the interest of being objective, not everyone had a positive opinion of Sparks, their music and their live performance style. It wasn't to everyone's taste. It didn't stop Sparks from being successful overall in 1974 but for the purpose of balance, the following is a bad review. Their performance at the Rainbow in London was reviewed in *Melody Maker* in July 1974:

> "Seldom can a band have had such encouragement from critics and audiences alike and been so dismal on the big night as were Sparks at the Rainbow on Sunday. The tedium fell like fine drizzle on the seats around me in the circle, and well before the end people were sloping off in whatever direction offered something that approached entertainment. In short, lethargy was running at a new high.
>
> Maybe, as their defenders will assert, they have been pushed too fast and too soon, but all the same, they delivered next to nothing. What seems on the records to be a minor masterpiece of wit and invention, emerged on stage as a tinny cabaret act, a gimmick pushed to extremes. Singer Russell Mael has an interesting and penetrating

falsetto that works well on the album, where the songs generally sound strong enough to complement him, but in live performance that piercing shriek going on ad infinitum really gets up your ass.

His performance, furthermore, isn't helped by some of the most banal patter between songs since the formation of Wakefield Theatre Club. Something on the lines of "now here's one called..." blah blah. He should really try to learn something about audience-handling. It's one thing to play Stockport Town Hall, and another to get yourself across at London's most critical venue. There were times when I had to remind myself they were bill-topping in the capital and not just a band getting out of the youth club circuit.

Another pointer is that their act is terribly one-paced. There's no build up, no climax, no effort to create any atmosphere — numbers begin, end and start again as if switches are being pulled every three minutes. But what totally put the mockers on their performance was the atrocious sound balance that steamrolled the melody and obliterated the lyrics, a crucial factor in the band's makeup. Apparently they had the same problem at the Cambridge Corn Exchange on an earlier gig so obviously this is another area to be worked at. Without lyrics, Sparks are charmless.

As a final criticism, the band's appearance doesn't

quite gel. Ron, with his monomanic (sic) stare, and Russell — English-style skinny-ribbed fop — are interesting to look at, but the rest of the band are nowhere. Intentional or not on the part of the Mael brothers, the four Anglo members are kept out of the spotlight. Someone should try and give them some kind of identity. If Island Records are going to have an out-and-out pop band, they might as well go all the way.

Perhaps though, the real mistake has been committed by some critics, who have larded Sparks with pretentions to freshness and sophistication that might well not be there. Something about the New Age of Innocence etc. That's unfortunate but it can't be helped. In the comparative absence of heroes we're all looking around for different names and faces. What I saw on Sunday was a pop band struggling to make some impression outside of the studio. I think they'll eventually make it. I'm told they already have. But honestly, the gig sucked.

The journalist did make a good point about how, aside from the Mael brothers, the rest of the band weren't really given much recognition or time in the spotlight. The whys and wherefores behind such decision aren't really clear but essentially, the fact that it happened didn't go unnoticed. In truth, Russell's voice has always had moments of sounding very different live to what it does on record. But does this warrant a review as bad as the latter? Probably not. It's interesting that there was an element of hype with regards to Sparks. The speed at which they broke the UK was such that there could have been something of an image and reputation to live up to when it came to going on tour. After their famous performance of 'This Town Ain't Big Enough For Both Of Us' on *Top Of The Pops*, Sparks had really made a name of themselves. Touring though, it's a totally different arena to *Top Of The Pops*, isn't it. It's ultimately a situation of the live versus the synthetic (as in, artists could safely mime along to a recorded track and didn't have to take any responsibility for crowd management on the latter).

Overall, Sparks' time in the UK must have been a whirlwind of enjoying a positive and sometimes frenzied welcome from fans (John Hewlett was quoted in *Sounds* in July 1974: "It's really weird. There are guys and girls around nineteen and twenty reacting like teeny boppers"). Also, considering the Mael brothers' passion for the country as self-confessed Anglophiles, it's great to think that they probably had a great time of it enjoying some of the more relaxed elements of the tour too. Everyone needs a day at the beach, right? It was reported in *Melody Maker* in June 1974: "Friday was hot and just like a day at the seaside should be except that most of Cleethorpes' promenade seemed shut. Still, Ron had a go on the Dalek machine and Russell went on the Super Bunny and they had their photos taken and bought lots of rock in the shape of kippers. Adrian's fetish for water-pistols was satisfied by buying six and Ian bought three and a battle which lasted out the day began. Ice cream and autographs. Souvenirs. It's that old tourist mentality again."

It comes across that the Mael brothers were probably feeling on top of the world to be in England, or at least a little starstruck by it. Ron was quoted in *Sounds* in June 1974: "We still aren't sure that we're in England." To which Russell was quoted: "We really don't know what's happening, it's all so confusing. There's no logical reason why this should be happening at this time because we've had other singles before and we've had albums before."

It wasn't long after finishing their first tour of Britain in 1974 that another one was planned. Dates for a second round of British touring were announced as early as August 1974 in *Melody Maker*: "Sparks hits the road again this autumn! The band embark on a month-long series of concert dates in November — their second British tour this year. And the new Sparks album, *Propaganda*, will be released to coincide with the opening concerts."

Radio & Records reported in October 1974:

Native Born Sparks Find Success In UK... Two young American brothers have taken London by storm with their group being voted "Most Talented Newcomers" by *Melody Maker*. The brothers are Ron and Russ Mael and their group is called Sparks. The group has had three top ten singles and a number one album in the UK, with a new single release coming out in the States called 'Talent Is An Asset' on Island Records.

Ron and Russ look like a before and after commercial for "The Dry Look". Ron sports a slicked down, patent leather wet head, vest, baggy pants and padded shoulder jacket with Russ looking like everyone's idea of a rock star appropriately decked out in long (and dry) hair, tight pants and glitter t-shirt. The incongruous twosome evidently triggered a sexual response in England with mobs of Londoners waiting after every performance to rip and tear off the group's clothes.

However, American fans are in conspicuous absence — a situation the group hopes to reverse with US TV appearances slated for fall review on *The Midnight Special, In Concert* and *Don Kirschner's Rock Concert*. The brothers are native Californians and attended UCLA while trying to get Sparks off the ground. The group decided to migrate to England hoping their special sound would have more appeal with the Europeans. The decision was, obviously, the right one with the group's only complaint being the weather and a lack of American hamburgers, hotdogs and milkshakes. Said Russ, "when we come home, we love to dine out in hamburger joints, even the hotel coffee shops are a treat."

Sparks is planning a US tour this January coming of the heels of a two-month European tour. After listening to the album, the sound of Sparks is unique and completely different than any rock 'n' roll to come along in years. It is understandable why the British love the group and it remains to be seen if their American cousins will follow suit.

Back in America, *Kimono My House* did make some kind of impact, albeit a small one. It got to one hundred and one in the *Billboard* chart. By mid 1974, for Sparks, Britain was still the place to be.

Chapter Five

Propaganda

Kimono My House had shown that Sparks could cut it in terms of pop music. Their musical potential in such field had already been hinted at in their earlier work on the tracks 'Wonder Girl' and 'High C' but with focussed management and a well organised British line-up behind them, the Mael brothers were elevated to new commercial heights via *Kimono My House*. The album had fitted in well with what was already going on in the charts from the likes of Roxy Music and David Bowie but equally, it didn't get lost in the shadows of what other artists were doing because clearly, Sparks were unique; melodically, lyrically, vocally and in terms of their image overall. Whether or not Sparks' image was manufactured is open to debate but either way, the fact is that *Kimono My House* and in particular, 'This Town Ain't Big Enough For Both Of Us', had opened doors for the band that made a second album with Island a natural choice of progression for all concerned. By the second half of 1974, such was the universal popularity of Sparks that they were featured on the covers of magazines aimed at younger audiences. This included *Mirabelle*, *Look-In* and in 1975, *Jackie*.

Half a year after the release of *Kimono My House*,

Propaganda followed. It was successful in the UK and the US. Commercially, *Propaganda* put Sparks in an excellent position internationally, because in the UK it carried on with what *Kimono My House* had started and in the US it functioned as the springboard that the Mael brothers needed for being able to continue as successful musicians in their home country. *Propaganda* got to number nine in the UK and to number sixty-three in the US.

The singles from *Propaganda*, 'Never Turn Your Back On Mother Earth' and 'Something For The Girl With Everything' weren't as successful as the ones from *Kimono My House* but really, the differences were marginal in the grand scheme of things; in the UK, the singles got to number thirteen and number seventeen respectively. In France, instead of 'Something For The Girl With Everything', 'Propaganda' paired with 'At Home, At Work, At Play' was released as a single. 'Achoo' was the only song from the *Propaganda* album to be released as a single in the US.

The first single from *Propaganda*, 'Never Turn Your Back On Mother Earth', was released in the UK in October 1974. Russell was quoted in *Sounds* in January 1975: "When we released 'Never Turn Your Back On Mother Earth' as a single we thought it was more conventional in a certain sort of way but by the fact that Sparks was doing it, it became strange."

It was performed on *Top Of The Pops* and then repeated on a later edition of the programme – it was first shown on the 24th October and then again on the 7th November (it was on the 24th October that Queen did the iconic performance of their hit, 'Killer Queen', which got to number two). 'Alabamy Right' was on the B-side. As well as getting to number thirteen in the UK, it also got to number forty in Germany. 'Something For The Girl With Everything' (with

'Marry Me' on the B-side) got to number seventeen after it too was featured on *Top Of The Pops* twice. The B-side of the single, 'Marry Me' had originally been written for *Kimono My House* and a demo had been made of the song during those sessions ('Marry Me' and 'Alabamy Right' were both originally demos for *Kimono My House*). Both of Sparks' singles released in the UK from *Propaganda* featured B-sides that weren't on the LP.

Sparks had come an incredibly long way in such a short space of time. By November 1974, it was only six months earlier that they had performed 'This Town Ain't Big Enough For Both Of Us' on *Top Of The Pops* in May 1974.

As journalist Pete Makowski advocated in *Sounds* in September 1974, "The album titled *Propaganda* comes at a tender stage of their careers. Now that they've reached a certain peak of success they've got to sustain it and establish themselves."

When asked if they had been mindful of such a thing when recording *Propaganda*, Russell was quoted: "One thing that was really an aid to the whole thing (*Kimono My House*) was that it was our third album, because I think we would have been quite inhibited on our next one which is our fourth. It's the fourth as in the second, if you can see my meaning. We weren't worried about this album because we were so involved in it. I think if we stopped to think about it we might have got a bit nervous, but it turned out we just did it and we're really pleased with it. We've never been especially goal orientated 'cause we just can't operate that way, it's just sort of do your stuff and hope for the best."

Propaganda was certainly a worthy album to follow *Kimono My House*. It featured the same style of music that Sparks had come to fame with in the UK. Russell's high paced falsetto and Ron's staccato piano chording are as present as ever and particularly come to the fore on the track, 'Something For The Girl With Everything'.

Whilst *Kimono My House* had benefitted from over a year's worth of time to be made, only three months were budgeted for the writing and recording of *Propaganda*. Ron Mael was quoted of *Propaganda* in *Trouser Press* in July 1982: "(It) was incredibly hard because there was a lot of pressure. *Kimono* was incredibly popular in England, and we were under the microscope. Anything we did was going to be judged. We went into the studio with a lot of songs, but a bit scared. We kept thinking about The Beatles and their constant rise. We tried to make *Propaganda* a little more complex than *Kimono My House*."

Upon being asked how they felt about their new album, Russell was quoted in *Sounds* in September 1974: "On the other album we just went in and laid down the basic tracks so it would sound good with the band. On this LP we didn't approach it at all like that." Really, although *Propaganda* had a much shorter gestation period than *Kimono My House* and inevitably the nerves were probably there as a result, it may have been the case that when it came to making their second Island album, Sparks had the momentum, artistically and professionally, to be able to work effectively with confidence and speed.

A lot of thought certainly went into making *Propaganda*. Russell was quoted in *Beat Instrumental* in August 1974: "We were recording a single recently and we were sitting there, spending three hours getting a bass drum sound. I mean, we were totally absorbed in that. All of a sudden I stopped and said to myself, 'Wait a minute, what are we doing? We've been here for three hours worrying about a bass drum and what relevance has that bass drum to life in general?'"

Ron was quoted in response, "I mean, we spent £120 just getting that bass drum sound."

Russell: "Yeah, and then we stop and think, but it's important to us and it might help us, you rationalise in fact. The other time I stopped was coming back from Hamburg on a plane. It was a really horrible ride, we thought there was a bomb guy on the plane and everybody was ordered to take their seats and the plane started shaking and I got really frightened. At that time I asked myself 'Why do I have to fly on planes every day, there has to be something better in life than this.' I guess things could be a lot simpler in life but you rationalise and once again you think, yeah, but this is what I really want to do."

Pete Makowski considered in *Sounds* in September 1974: "If a commercially orientated swine were in Sparks' shoes, he would probably release many singles in the vein of 'This Town' which leads me on to tell you that the band's new single, 'Never Turn Your Back On Mother Earth' is totally diverse to what you've heard before, making it completely original and jolly good — which is something that has been Sparks' trait."

When asked if the single, 'Never Turn Your Back On Mother Earth' was intentionally different to the band's other releases, Ron was quoted in *Sounds* in September 1974: "It's just played at the wrong speed." Russell was quoted in the same feature as he offered a more expansive answer: "It wasn't done intentionally as a single, the same goes for the other two. This one wasn't done as a single, it was just done as another song. There were a lot of possibilities on the new LP that could have been the next single and that we did think about. It wasn't the thought like 'let's do something different from the other two singles. It was just one of those songs and everyone said it was a single and we were keen on the idea. We really like the element of surprise." Ron's was quoted as he interjected: "The element of committing suicide."

Kimono My House and *Propaganda* sit together well as Sparks' two 1974 albums. Really, musically, they are not too different from each other and it could be argued that any track from *Kimono My House* wouldn't sound out of place on *Propaganda* and vice versa. The pressure that may have been felt during the making of *Propaganda* is arguably not evident in the music and considering that the album had to be made in a lot less time than *Kimono My House* was, it stands alone as a damn good album and generally, many reviews are reflective of that. Russell was quoted in *Sounds* in September 1974: "A lot of people who have heard the new album have said it really sounds like a combination of our first three LPs. It's got the hardness of *Kimono* but then has a bit of the – whatever the elements were in the first two albums, a bit of that flavour but more aggressive. A lot of people say that."

Propaganda was recorded at AIR studios in August 1974. Recording began very soon after Sparks' first tour of the UK that year. The record was produced by Muff Winwood and the band consisted of the same line-up as those who had toured with the Maels just before; on lead guitar was Adrian Fisher, Trevor White was on rhythm guitar, Ian Hampton was on bass and Dinky Diamond was on drums.

It wasn't long after recording *Propaganda* that Fisher was out of the band and it was around this time that Brian May was asked to join. It was reported in *Sounds* in September 1974: "The band have recently lost the services of guitarist Adrian Fisher." Russell was quoted: "We let Adrian have his release from the band, to put it mildly we kicked Adrian out of the band. We're just at the point in our careers, we're not exactly sure whether we're going to carry on as a five piece. We may add a guitarist but we're not sure what we're going to do. If we're going to have an extra guitar player he's going to be one contributing something more in the vein of Sparks as opposed to a more traditional style of guitar player – and we just thought this was the time to make a bit of a change."

Of course, Brian declined the Mael's offer. Whether he did so explicitly or through a lack of further discussion with the brothers isn't clear but really, maybe it's one of those "everything happens for a reason" kind of things. Sparks would have sounded very different with Brian May on board and more so, perhaps, May had yet to make his next album with Queen, *A Night At The Opera*, which of course features one of Queen's most essential songs, 'Bohemian Rhapsody'. Russell was quoted in *The Quietus* in August 2017: "At one time during the seventies, Queen had done one tour of America and things weren't really happening for them in a big way just yet. We met with Brian May and just said, 'We have a position open for a guitar player.' It was maybe being entertained but I don't know to what extent. We had meetings with him but it obviously didn't work out that way."

It was during the recording of *Kimono My House* that Ron stopped using a Farfisa organ (he had used one on Sparks' first two albums on Bearsville) and instead chose to use the RMI Electra piano. He opted to continue with the RMI Electra piano for the recording of *Propaganda*. It was when he moved to London at the end of 1973 that he purchased the instrument. It was one of the models with three sounds; piano, organ and harpsichord.

However, the extent to which the piano sound was a bit too on the synthetic side of things inspired some interesting innovation. Ron ran the RMI Electra piano through a Maestro

Echoplex. It was basically a portable tape delay that used real tape. It is plausible that this may have been what added the haunting, slightly echoing sound to the keyboard-based parts on (for instance) 'This Town Ain't Big Enough For Both Of Us' and 'B.C.'.

Every track on *Propaganda* was written by Ron alone. The exceptions are 'Reinforcements', 'Thanks But No Thanks' and 'Bon Voyage', all of which Ron co-wrote with Russell. As short as the album's opening title track is, a lot of work went into it. Russell's voice was overdubbed many times over. A longer version that was all still acapella was recorded but Muff Winwood decided that a shorter version would be best, to which the rest of the band agreed.

'Propaganda'was initially intended to be an acoustic guitar track but it evolved with vocals on the basis that the band found it easier than working out extra guitar parts. It could be said that the album's opening track sounds as it does due to ergonomics rather than creative intention, but either way, it offers something that is technically sound in terms of vocal harmony. In such regard, it's fascinating and certainly attention grabbing.

When it came to how best to work innovatively, not everyone agreed with everything though. Trevor White was quoted in *Goldmine* in July 1995: "'Achoo' ended with this really great characteristic long solo (from Adrian Fisher) and they wiped it off and put on all those horrid multi-tracked sneezes. They figured everyone had heard a guitar solo, but they hadn't heard us all sneezing."

Pete Makowski reviewed *Propaganda* in *Sounds* in November 1974:

So now we have the second offering from the band since their success on the Island label. Hmmm, it's a little deeper than *Kimono*. The first two albums in the band's Bearsville days took on two separate directions while this one is development on the style of *Kimono*. The arrangements are more interesting, not so obvious, still entertaining. It seems the band have found a happy medium between their eccentricity and commercialism (an odd combination).

The album opens with the title track acapella style which leads into 'At Home, At Work, At Play' which has that migraine pounding beat. Right now, I prefer side two which opens up with 'Never Turn Your Back On Mother Earth' which I'm sure you're all familiar with. This is followed by the song that was going to be the band's follow up to 'Amateur Hour' – 'Something For The Girl With Everything' which has Russell singing at lightning fast pace. 'Achoo' has a kind of perverted Charleston melody with lyrics like "Who knows what the wind's going to bring when the invalids sing" – this is all new to me. 'Who Don't Like Kids' is in that bouncy vein. The side closes with 'Bon Voyage' which reveals a very toonful (sic) side to the band – this is a composition by both brothers.

The album explores the production possibilities of the band. Russ's vocals are overdubbed which make them an instrument on their own. Ron uses

Mellotron, creating an interesting sound. I think this album will take a few more listenings. Still, they say the ones that cut deeper last longer.

In an interview with *New Musical Express* in November 1974, Ron revealed that he wrote the music before the lyrics. He was quoted: "There's no problem getting the words to fit." He was quoted of his influences in the same feature: "I enjoy Porter, Noel Coward, Van Dyke Parks too — I like short things, like a lot of those early sixties American singles, garage band stuff, 'cause you felt that those guys were your peers. I don't like the tortured artist syndrome. The thing about a good lyric is that you can make the trivial become important. Also playing live, the fact that it's in there is significant — the songs aren't just vehicles for boogieing."

That said, on days where there was even more of a creative flow, Ron's writing process followed a slightly different order. He was quoted in *Sounds* in June 1974: "When God is really on our side, the lyrics come at the same time as the music."

John Peel reviewed the 'Never Turn Your Back On Mother Earth' single in *Sounds* in October 1974: "Oh yes! Very, very nice. This exhilarating oeuvre is taken from the impending *Propaganda* LP. If you wish to place your order today then the number will be ILPS 9312. I'll wait for a moment while you nip down the shop to order it. Okay? I think you've done the right thing. The side opens and closes with a morsel of harpsichord — perhaps, as both records have been produced by Muff 'And What A Man' Winwood, the self-same harpsichord that appeared on the Sutherland Brothers and Quiver single. By now you should be familiar with the sort of noise that Sparks make. Personally I think it's one of the great rock sounds — enduring, completely their own and teen-terrific through and through. On 'Mother Earth' they move at a slightly more sedate pace than on their previous two biggies, advising us as they go, in reference to Mother Earth, 'don't be tempted by her favours'. True, true. There's a slight Magical Mystery sequence in the middle somewhere. Also a spot of tuneful lead guitar. Must do battle with Rod and Roxy Music (q.v.) for the very tippy top of the charts. The B-side, 'Alabamy Right', is spot on also. It's a brisker piece, ornamented with some nifty piano and some hand clapping that clearly came up the river from New Orleans and could be heard for twelve miles across the Delta on a still night. If you fail to add this to your collection then my agents will pass among you with flails and instruments of war."

Prior to declaring the keyboard as his main instrument, Ron played guitar for eight years due to playing keyboards being seen as "really pansy". He was quoted in *Sounds* in December 1974: "I don't consider myself a guitarist but I know the chords and I know enough to write on it — and to entertain people at parties." In the same feature, it was revealed that Ron wrote 'Never Turn Your Back On Mother Earth' on the guitar. He was quoted: "Sometimes I really like writing a song that in a way isn't being written by you, it's putting yourself in the place of songwriter so it doesn't sound like something you've done. I think it's less flowing on piano, more rigid, a lot more staccato and in a way a lot more melodic on guitar."

By November 1974, Sparks were very popular indeed and merchandising was part and parcel of how marketable they were. By this point, the back pages of *New Musical Express* contained an advert for people to place orders for Sparks scarves. They were available in blue, white or gold at 60p each. Also available were pin badges at 30p each and chrome I.D. bracelets at 75p each. Engraving options were

"Ron and Russ", "Sparks" or "I Luv Sparks".

It was reported in *Sounds* in July 1974: "Joseph Fleury runs Sparks' fan club and has been doing so since he met them at Greenwich Village over a year ago." Fleury's fanzine went by the name of *Sparks Flashes*. Sparks were actively involved with the fanzine and sometimes contributed towards it as part of having a good rapport with Fleury. Ron contributed a tongue in cheek list of ten things that needed to be in place to write good songs. The list of instructions stated:

1) Avoid the key of E. Avoid the key of A.

2) Never use a major or minor when an augmented or diminished will do just as well.

3) Experiment with arresting chord sequences. Surely there's been a chord sequence that you felt was maybe just a bit too kinky, a bit too complicated. Use it.

4) Never repeat anything.

5) Try adding a small nine, eleven or thirteen randomly after a few chords in the song.

6) Save your cleverest lyrics for those long passages in one chord.

7) A good rule of thumb is, "When a solo soon will grate, modulate."

8) When a solo does creep in, a gripping spoken part over-the-top can usually attract the lion's share of attention.

9) Wherever possible all solos should be restricted to the final passage of a song where they can be quickly and cleanly faded.

10) Reminder, it's never too late. One inch of splicing tape and a sharp razor blade can eliminate a multitude of sins.

Fleury's Sparks fan club membership grew as rapidly

as Sparks' success did in 1974. As a result, the admin side of things went a bit wild. He was quoted in *Sounds* in July 1974: "The mail's quadrupled in the last few weeks. When I first started the club we had about two hundred members, now it's getting to the thousands."

It was then reported in *Sounds* in November 1974: "Sparks' Fan Club Fizzles Out – This week brings another tale of woe about fan clubs. It's the Sparks' club this time. Lindsay Warren, a reader in Chepstow, phones us in desperation. She sent £1 in June for membership of the club and since then has written four letters asking when she would see something for her money. Until now she has had no reply from the club, not even an acknowledgement. When the club started in this country there were glowing reports on how it was handled – the quarterly booklets produced were informative, attractive and well worth the fans' subscription money. Joseph Fleury, who has been running the club since its inception, started by replying personally to every letter. But there is a limit to the amount of fan mail one person can handle and when the membership grew past the one thousand mark, it became impossible to deal with it efficiently. Added to this, Mr Fleury spent part of the summer in the States and during his absence the fan mail was completely unattended. The backlog is being cleared now and a mailing is due to go out within the next two weeks." It must have been annoying for all of the people waiting for correspondence but still, it is certainly testament to the extent that Sparks' career gained momentum in 1974.

Makowski considered in *Sounds* in September 1974: "The lightning fast rise to fame for Sparks has been quite an enigma. I mean their debut hit single wasn't instantly appealing in a commercial sense and their excellent *Kimono*

My House album has been riding high in the charts since its release, which means they are no one hit wonders. The Mael brothers are a commercial success, something they undoubtedly deserve, leaving a lot of bewildered critics puzzled. The band have stayed in the background since their sell-out tour, and the brothers have been travelling around the world promoting themselves. Now they are back with a new album, single and tour which leaves an everyday journalist like myself with so many questions to ask them. I spoke to the brothers at Island's Basing Street Offices where they were listening, with keen interest, to the B-side of their new single with fan club secretary Joseph Fleury. Ron and Russell were, as per usual, impeccably dressed and generally seemed to be in a good mood."

The cover art on *Propaganda* really brings it home that Sparks was (and very much still is!) Ron and Russell's band. That said, it was the first Sparks album cover to feature just the brothers on the front. With their first two Bearsville albums, the brothers were featured with the rest of the band at the time. *Propaganda*, Sparks' second album in Island, was the first to feature the brothers on the cover. Regional variations of the album artwork included French and Italian releases with gatefold covers; the UK release simply contained the record in an inner sleeve.

As with *Kimono My House*, *Propaganda* didn't have the name of the band printed on the front cover of the album. Equally, these was no title on there either. Instead, both of Sparks' albums in 1974 were identifiable with stickers that were used when both albums were first sold in the shops.

The Mael brothers are tied and captive on a speedboat on the front cover. On the back cover, they are in a similarly compromising scenario in the back of a car. The cover art on *Propaganda* is certainly different to what *Kimono My House* was but it is no less eccentric. The back cover of *Propaganda* features the rest of the band stood outside of the car (a Humber) as they look menacingly at their captives (this image was used by bootleggers in the nineties and used as a front cover for a CD by the name of *One And A Half Nelson*). And what became of the garage in which the photo was shot? Well, Russell was quoted in *Record Collector* in July 2003: "Westbourne Grove – there's a little strip of shops and that garage. It's funny to see a now-defunct Heron Garage. That could be me in the car while my dad was filling up." To which Ron was quoted, "That's novel – we've outlasted a product. It's usually the other way round. Nostalgic because of the product rather than us!"

The predicaments that the Mael brothers were featured in on *Propaganda*'s album art isn't too far from truth. The image on the front of the album was shot on the south coast of Sussex where the brothers really were bound and gagged whilst sat uncomfortably on a speedboat. Russell was quoted in fanzine, *Sparks News* (volume nineteen, number six): "We shot this on the south coast of England in a gale force wind. That look in our eyes is not acting! We were freezing! The photographer had originally suggested that we be bound and gagged and dropped from an airplane with parachutes on, and he would photograph us from the air as he too descended. We declined his kind offer."

The inner sleeve photograph of Ron and Russell tied up on a bed next to a telephone was used, in black and white, as the cover for the 'Achoo' single released in the US. All of the photography on *Propaganda*, including the design concept, was the brainchild of Monty Coles – an Australian photographer who was working in England at the time. In 1977, he worked on the Bryan Ferry album, *In Your Mind* (also released on Island Records). The design for Ferry's album was given the go ahead from Nicholas Deville, who had also been active with the design element of Sparks' *Kimono My House* album. Coles later went back to Australia, where he built a successful career as a fashion photographer.

In response to claims that Sparks' image was one of decadence, Ron was quoted in *New Musical Express* in November 1974: "Maybe around the *Woofer* period there was something perverse or strange in the songs but it isn't a deliberate theme now. Actually, the purpose of the album cover pose was merely to be eye catching and not to reflect the lyrics."

Propaganda was reviewed in *New Musical Express* in October 1974:

> People whose tastes are rooted in the blues did not, apparently, find what Ron Mael was doing with rock on *Kimono My House* either interesting or appealing. Okay. They will find the situation unchanged by *Propaganda*, which, for them, will presumably appear as wilfully daft as ever. People who, on the other hand, found something entertaining or creative in the Maels' music last time around can rest assured that that something has not departed — even if there's less of it available on the new album. Some of the tricks have "worn thin" and the rather dense, inaccurate production can sometimes hide the new tricks which were, one presumes, part of the artistic justification for recording another album (the commercial justifications are manifest). Specifically, Ron Mael's compositional formula of a harmonically and rhythmically bizarre verse resolved by a stamping chorus on which all beats

are equal and the melody "doubles" the root
note of each successive chord – that's definitely
wearing thin. Also, the on-beat clapping here is
over-employed, giving the effect of a posturing
preciousness that is, unsurprisingly, confirmed
in the lyrics in general. 'Who Don't Like Kids' is,
for example, headed for the whole "diminutive
charm" number that Bolan eventually descended
into – and one does begin to lose patience with
the Maels' demure and capricious affectations.
On *Kimono*, the lyrics – even when ironic or
apparently superficial – still retain a distinct
substantiality which over-spilled from something
obviously possessed of a degree of depth (e.g.
'Thank God It's Not Christmas') into what might
otherwise have seemed trivial ('Here In Heaven')
or wilfully inscrutable ('Equator').

So – are the Maels merely dissembling, or are they
ultimately of no real substance at all? I think they
have substance – but what that substance is might
only be becoming clear in *Propaganda*. Which
is: decadence. Not the counterfeit of decadence
employed as a focus by people like Lou Reed and
The New York Dolls, but the decadence of the
elitist in-bred – which I suppose, finds its nether
reaches in the Upper Class Twit syndrome. The
Maels aren't twits, but they do appear disposed to
perversity as if it were a growing concern in itself.
And when such a delusion finds itself encouraged,
the trivial can easily become confused with the
observation of the trivial. The social whirl of the
upper class East Coast American boy forms the

backdrop to *Propaganda* with a couple of related themes employed as specific pegs from which to hang a point of view, e.g. Girls as in "twenty first birthday party" and Family as in "whose cousin are you?" or "his father's an oil millionaire" (examine songs like 'B.C.' and 'Who Don't Like Kids' to see what I'm driving at).

The Maels' attitude to girls is particularly illuminating. The girl takes the male role of dominance and voracity while Russell becomes submissive, helpless, tightly cross-legged and demure. A point of view echoed in the sleeve art. Thus numbers like 'Something For The Girl With Everything' ("You can breathe another day/Secure in knowing she won't break you — yet!"), 'At Home, At Work, At Play' ("Stop, she's unique especially at home/Where you're butler maid and often cook") and 'Don't Leave Me Alone With Her' ("A Hitler wearing heels/A soft Simon Legree/A hun with honey skin/De Sade who makes good tea"). Not only are the subjects more delightedly superficial, the work that's gone into discussing them is too. About the only really interesting couplet in a very wordy lyric sheet comes from 'Thanks But No Thanks' ("My parents say the world is cruel/I think that they prefer it cruel"). Apart from that, the general level of penetration is about as shallow as the torturous use of military vernacular in a romantic context on 'Reinforcements'. Of course, it's a joke about songs like that, trouble is, this time out, it is a song like that.

Propaganda has charm (if you wish to be charmed). It has bags of "variety", there are plenty of "tunes". Parts of it are quite as good as *Kimono My House* and there are even a few advances (the operatic sarcasms of the closer, 'Bon Voyage', for example). It depends on how you want to take it. By itself, who knows? Perhaps fairly amusing. In the context of previous work and everything else, well, I'm going to keep *Kimono* and Ivor Cutler's album, which you'll find reviewed somewhere near here.

That's quite the review there! Essentially, the journalist's take on *Propaganda* was that the lyrics get kinky in places and musically he prefers *Kimono My House*. For what it's worth, in his review of *Propaganda*, the journalist was very accurate in how he described what's going on with the handclaps and the rhythm in general. However, whilst he advocates that it gets a bit samey on *Propaganda*, it is an opinion that is very open to debate; many would argue that Sparks had a distinctively enjoyable signature sound on *Kimono My House* and that it was not lost on *Propaganda* either. Really, the review of *Propaganda* in *New Musical Express* in October 1974 is a good one in that, historically, it is very demonstrative of how a lot of people took Sparks at the time and indeed now. They are a very Marmite band and arguably, that's part of their (as the reviewer may have put it) charm.

Propaganda was reviewed in the *Acton Gazette* in December 1974:

These Mael brothers certainly are a weird pair. Ron looks like a youthful Adolf Hitler sitting silently at the piano and glaring into the distance, while Russell has a voice like a comic opera singer and could be Marc Bolan's double.

By switching the focus of their music from guitars to all manner of keyboards and putting lots of echo on the vocals, they have come up with a very usual sound that has made them stand out from the rest. Consequently, this is an album with a variety that makes for interesting listening. But breaking new musical ground is never easy and there are times when the brothers' ideas don't really work. The arrangements just get too complicated and a certain amount of dull repetition begins to creep in. For example, there are traces of 'This Town Ain't Big Enough For Both Of Us' on several of these tracks and the same musical themes are recycled several times.

So the album still leaves it to be seen whether the Maels can keep coming up with the original ideas or whether they are going to make the mistake of relying on established ones.

I advocate that this is a strange review because it includes some strong opinions that the reviewer doesn't go on to substantiate. For instance, they complain that several of the tracks on *Propaganda* contain traces of 'This Town Ain't Big Enough For Both Of Us' but they don't list the instances in which they feel this is the case. Are they referring to instrumentation, melody, structure?

I'm not trying to be facetious purely because as a Sparks fan, of course I hold an extent of bias, but really, it's actually quite difficult to see what the reviewer is getting at — especially in terms of how they complain that Sparks isn't original. Wow! Really? However, moving on from my own bias as a fan, the review is interesting in that it is demonstrative of how people who really didn't get into Sparks' music may have just felt that all of their tracks sounded too alike. Eccentric musicians always walk a fine line between having cult success and irritating listeners who can't, or won't, see beyond the eccentricity and really, that is an endearing aspect of Sparks' image and indeed, success.

Besides, as the *Bucks Examiner* advocated in December 1974: "Russell Mael's weird falsetto guaranteed Sparks a degree of individuality when they hit the pop scene. It was a gimmick which could so quickly have faded, but imaginative writing by Russell and brother Ron have maintained the band's magnetic originality. *Propaganda* was in the same crazy vein as their early single hits and whether or not you like their nerve-jangling style you have got to admire their ability to sound so different from everyone else. It is a high-power performance from the off with every track a winner as the boys rock, bounce and swing through eleven numbers. Witty, weird and wonderful."

It was reported in *Record World* in September 1974: "Sparks tour the UK from November 2nd, the day after their *Propaganda* album is released. A single taken from the LP is released two days later – 'Never Turn Your Back On Mother Earth', written by Ron Mael."

New Musical Express reported in November 1974:

Things couldn't really have got off to a worse start for Sparks. First their coach broke down in Barnsley – of all places – which necessitated everyone clambering aboard an antediluvian traction bus. Then there were the highly necessary and expensive additions to the equipment which arrived at the very last moment. It wasn't exactly peaches and limousines.

Our hostelry in York, the scene of the beginning of the lengthy forty day tour, is one of those B.R. "grand hotel" jobs complete with massive lounge and huge double-well staircase that Garbo could descend all the way down without ever reaching the bottom. Unfortunately, the management aren't yet attuned to the coming of rock and roll to York — they're characteristically blunt (rude, if you like), although it's hard to envisage a more inoffensive bunch than Sparks.

The brothers Mael, band, and tour manager John Hewlett are at lunch sampling the delights of a not unadventurous lad while surveying a decidedly pretty but wet view. These are the hinterlands alright, only the landscaped lawns are sodden rather than plush. The waiter hovers, a genuine Heathcliff lookalike — dark, satanic and decidedly bemused. None of the staff seem prepared for the excitement, even though a growing number of female devotees are assembling within the confines of the lobby. They've been there since 11am, will remain until the gig, returning when the band departs on Sunday for Newcastle. And guess what? They're going to see them there too, and Liverpool and Leicester. Loyalty is hardly an explanation for such faith in the cause. It's either fanaticism or madness or consummate proof that Sparks are a major force to rank with the best of Britain.

If you think touring is remotely connected or enhanced by relaxation, forget it. Even gourmets must check out the proverbial sound, which means that for Sparks too, business definitely comes before pleasure and all troop off to Central Hall for a thorough technical run-through which renders sightseeing impossible. Free time is minimal to the extent of being mythical. When they return to base, the encroaching tension seems to affect everyone equally. First night nerves aren't overly apparent but Ron, Russell and Ian Hampton become increasingly quiet. Only Dinky Diamond and Trevor White maintain a constant flow of chirpy chatter. Perhaps they are oblivious of the evening's significance, or maybe they're just better at hiding it.

Sparks' performance in York was reviewed in *New Musical Express* in November 1974:

Central Hall is situated close by the scenic artificial lake in University grounds. Inside, support band Pilot are playing the ideal warm up set, accomplished enough to keep the audience happy, yet aware of who they've really come to see. The sold-out notices are up by eight o'clock. Fourteen hundred people banked tightly together, anticipating collectively. During the interval, selections from Walt Disney soundtracks keep everyone amused, a fantasia of crazy tunes tailor-made for preparatory entertainment. The crowd is animated and growing restless.

Suddenly, the lights are dimmed and the band troop out to deafening applause. The Maels emerge last. Brother Ron lopes towards his seat wearing oh-so-formal threads which have made him the Franchot Tone of rock. Mael junior takes up a side-stage position in total darkness until a spotlight singles him out and it's straight into 'Propaganda', fifty seconds of the most bizarre pronunciation, practically spoken by Russell in one of his lower ranges. Considering that no-one's heard the new album yet it could be interpreted as a risky opening but 'Talent Is An Asset' is a safe throw.

Ron fixes the audience with a variety of unnerving stares. He's cultivated a particularly mean sideways look, guaranteed to send shivers up your spine. He has this uncanny charisma on stage which makes him an essential focal point even though he's practically static. In 'B.C.' (another new number in which an idyllic family situation retrogresses to prehistoric instability) he stabs the keyboards with rare relish, lending the melody an insistent music hall quality and gazing with disdainful disapprobation at the cavortings (sic) of his fraternal sibling. 'Thank God It's Not Christmas' and 'In My Family' are infinitely more powerful live than on *Kimono*, anyway, they have the added advantage of the visual mystique with which Sparks infuse the show. Russell, sporting a neat cravat, flits constantly across the boards, demure as little white riding hood. He retains a wistful demeanour even when singing the most cynical or sharp lyric.

The feature continued:

White's rhythm and Hampton's faultless bass are a revelation. Both ex members of Jook, a perfect rapport already exists between them so that the whole band is now amazingly tight. Momentary disaster struck when Ron's foot pedal broke down; he could either extract the necessary chords at maximum volume or not at all. Lesser personalities might have been dismayed — he just picked up the faulty object and dashed it to the floor, grinning maliciously.

'Reinforcements' is a great number for Dinky to display his prowess at the drums. Throughout the concert he grew in stature, becoming increasingly impressive with the cleanest breaks, rolls and cymbal tapping you'll hear in a long time. Now truly established, he contributes more urgency and invention without ever being annoyingly showy. Actually the whole act is precise and distinctive, the group's confidence emanating from the mutual understanding evolved at stringent rehearsals.

'Who Don't Like Kids' was introduced at some length by Russell who conveyed some of the cutting sarcasm nestling within the words, anything but sentimental. His stage manner, however, is so endearing that favourable relations with the audience are immediately established. Besides, no-one else has a voice like that. While brother Ron glowers fiendishly he perches on a stool and briefly delineates the magnum opus 'Bon Voyage', a tear-jerking tribute to the animals that get left off the ark, delivered very tongue in cheek.

The music here breaks new ground for Sparks. Ron's excellently understated synthesiser line and Trevor's torn off solo severed the acoustics in unison. The febrile pace is restored with "Hasta Mañana Monseiur", always a zippy number.

Also from the same feature:

You don't realise exactly how fast the act is until you see them. Russell covers enough ground to qualify for the Boston Red Sox but still doesn't break sweat — that's true style. On *Propaganda*, 'Achoo' sounds a trifle fey but tonight it works. Our hero sneezes gracefully and all are enchanted. From here on, a strong position became invincible and the enthusiasm which the new material received was phenomenal. On 'Don't Leave Me Alone With Her' Ron got down and got with it in his own inimitable way, that insane two finger organ style dictated a very heavy middle eight. A scintillating 'Never Turn Your Back On Mother Earth' and a riotous 'Amateur Hour' brought the strange conglomeration of students and local kids to its feet. Not only were the long-standing fans satisfied, those hearing Sparks for the first time reacted favourably too.

It was a pity that rather arbitrary security did its best to subdue them when the excitement was at its height. The behaviour of the bouncers during 'This Town' was unforgivable and prevented quite a harmless section of the audience from enjoying themselves.

Even so, the reception Sparks received was spontaneous thanks, later turning to delight when they encored. Russell had changed to natty red-rimmed shades and orange skiing anorak – a space-age Cary Grant with curls. During golden oldie 'Girl From Germany', his voice soared to a remarkable falsetto. The song is altogether more polished now than on the *Woofer* album and closing number, 'Here In Heaven', has an edge that surpasses the recorded version and shows how accomplished the whole group has become. Backstage, Hewlett is beaming "I said we'd only encore if they really asked for it – and they did." Scaling the perimeter of the hall proved a hazardous task as scores of aficionados mobbed the band, who seemed surprised by delighted at the adulation, their high spirits lasting tell the early hours."

It was reported of the last performance of the UK *Propaganda* tour in *Sounds* in December 1974: "The last night was at the California Ballroom, an excellent and extremely underrated venue that usually caters for soul bands and provides facilities that are undreamed of in the rest of Britain. This and the ultra-enthusiastic audience probably contributed to what turned out to be the finest Sparks concert I've ever seen. The band walked on to mucho thunderous applause."

Regarding Sparks' post-*Propaganda* tour of Britain, Russell was quoted in *Sounds* in January 1975: "It was a lot better on all fronts — the crowd reaction, our performance is a lot stronger, everything seems to have improved tenfold. I think we feel much more confident this time round because there's been a real acceptance of the band. On the last tour I think a lot of people came out of curiosity — 'who was that group who had a hit with a funny song?' or 'who was that funny man who plays keyboards?' — as opposed to people really coming out to see Sparks. There were some fans but it was really divided on the last tour."

Even once the curiosity had settled, Sparks continued to attract a diverse audience; teenyboppers and people who were genuinely there for the music itself. It was reported in *Sounds* in December 1974: "Tonight the screaming was persistent and drove calls of 'shaddup' and 'we wanna hear the music' from the people at the back."

Being in high demand probably required a lot of stamina. It was reported in *Sounds* in December 1974: "Sparks looked surprisingly fit and strong considering they've been doing gigs continuously for the past few weeks. Since their last tour they have become more unified... The new material sounds well worn in while some of the older numbers have had some slight new touches... Two pleasant surprises were 'Bon Voyage' and 'Never Turn Your Back On Mother Earth' which are totally different to the band's normally more percussive style and it gave everyone a chance to lay back a little and had the audience swaying from side to side. The band closed with 'This Town' and 'Amateur Hour', to which the whole hall virtually erupted and hundreds of kids streamed down to the front."

The extent of Sparks' international success is evident in

the television appearances that they made prior to the start of the tour they did for *Propaganda*. They were on German TV in late September. The set list for the *Propaganda* tour was an excellent showcase of Sparks at their best. It included songs from *Kimono My House* and *Propaganda* as well as 'Wonder Girl' and 'Girl From Germany' from their Bearsville days.

I strongly recommend the following as essential listening: *Sparks Live In The Studio*. It was broadcast on American FM Radio in September 1974. It is an excellent demonstration of, musically, where Sparks were at post *Kimono My House* and pre *Propaganda*. The songs from *Kimono My House* sound more polished and, on the whole, played with more energy than on the album. The songs that were due to be released on *Propaganda* strongly show the extent to which the band had their performances polished and ready long before the album was due to hit the shops. In between the songs, there are instances in which Russell offers some fascinating insights into the meanings behind some of the songs. He said of 'Here In Heaven'; "It's a suicide pact song. That's all it is." He said of 'Amateur Hour'; "It's (a) teenage frustration song, of some sorts."

Also: "For the first time on American radio, the extended version of 'This Town Ain't Big Enough For Both Of Us'... We stuck in an extra verse and an extra bridge on that one just to pad out our set." The whole recording is well worth a listen because it points towards what Sparks may have sounded like in some of the live gigs that I've quoted throughout this book.

Sparks did their first gig in France on 30th November 1974 at the Olympia Theatre in Paris. Russell was quoted in *Sounds* in January 1975: "I really enjoy Europe, there's a certain different feel that's not English at all and definitely not American and a lot of people say that the band sound continental. When we were in Paris last time we did some TV shows there and we played on a really middle of the road TV show and it was sort of accepted that way. In France, we're one of the French sort of bands and it's really strange that we're being accepted on the continent as continental boys. I don't know why it is."

A very short European tour for *Propaganda* also included dates in the Netherlands, Belgium and Germany. It was while in Paris that the Maels were introduced to the French film director, Jacques Tati. Russell was quoted in *Record Collector* July 2003: "We saw him working on the 1974 film *Parade* and met him in his office in Paris." The script Tati was working on was for a film by the title *Confusion*. Ron composed the title song for the film and the brothers were invited to have parts in it. It was reported in the *Daily Mirror* in March 1975: "Ron and Russell Mael, of the bizarre hit group Sparks, are to star in a film called *Confusion*. Sounds just their style."

Sadly though, it never came to be because Tati was taken ill. Russell was quoted of Tati in *Record Collector* July 2003: "He always thought that we could be a conduit to expand his audience at the time, and we obviously wanted to work with this cinema legend. It was really sad that he ended up dying relatively soon after that. He wasn't in the best of health."

The film was going to be the story of two American TV studio employees working for a rural French TV company. In an interview with *The Quietus* in August 2017, Ron was asked: "You once said your biggest regret was not being in a film with Jacques Tati. You were all set to star in a picture called *Confusion*, but ultimately his ill health meant it went unmade." Ron was quoted: "Yeah, it's really, even to this day, one of my biggest regrets. We were, and still are, huge fans of what Jacques Tati did as a filmmaker, and also just the struggles he had to go through to get films made. We were introduced to him by a guy from Island in Switzerland in the mid-seventies, and Tati came up with this idea, which seemed bizarre at the time, but kinda made sense after we sat back and thought about it for a while. We met several times in Paris with Tati, and there was a film that was going to be made about two American television people – a director and a technician who were gonna help out a struggling French TV company. The one thing that we can still take from that is meeting him, and just him walking into the room and it's M. Hulot, you know, and he has his kind of crumpled up mac and hat."

Russell was quoted: "We were also able to do one TV show in Stockholm with him. He was really popular in Sweden and knowing that this project was happening, they invited us to come and do something on TV with him. He wanted a horse and we went on and just kind of adlibbed stuff with a white horse... (we are) trying to locate these tapes because it was on Swedish national TV and no one seems to know where they are. We hope they'll turn up one day."

Propaganda had a later release date in America. *Cash Box* reported under the announcement of "Island Slates Six LPs For Jan" in January 1975: "*Propaganda*, Sparks' second album for Island, was produced by Muff Winwood and features all new Ron Mael compositions, including the current British single release, 'Never Turn Your Back On Mother Earth'." The other five albums listed in the report were *Taking Tiger Mountain (By Strategy)* by Eno, *Have You Heard This Story??* by Swamp Dogg, *Fear* by John Cale, *The End* by Nico and on Island's Mango label, the re-release of the soundtrack to

The Harder They Come by Jimmy Cliff.

In November 1974, *Melody Maker* reported under the headline of "Sparkless":

> Sparks are quitting Britain for a year! The current tour will be the band's last British dates until the winter of 1975 — apart from a special Christmas concert in Leeds. The band's decision has been forced by their heavy work schedule in the USA — they start their first major American tour in February and another series of US concert dates have been planned for the autumn.
>
> "We also want to record our next album in the States so it's a case of staying there for some time", Ron Mael told the *Melody Maker* this week, "besides, things are escalating for us in America — our *In Concert* TV show was shown there last week. So we just want to keep things going. The band will now be based wherever we happen to be at any one time."
>
> Sparks will also tour in Japan, Australia and Europe during 1975, prolonging the band's exile from Britain. Their new album, the third for Island Records, will be recorded in the spring. "We've done two albums in Britain and we've decided to try out new surroundings for the third. A change of environment will probably bring about subtle differences in the music", Mael said.
>
> The band's present British tour is scheduled to end at Dunstable's California Ballroom on November 28th, but a Christmas concert in Leeds

Town Hall is planned for December 20th. Tickets, all priced at £1.10, will be available from Barkers of Leeds on December 2nd. Sparks' decision to quit Britain however, is not related to the country's severe tax system – Mael insisted they are leaving purely because of their foreign work schedule. But Sparks will return next year for winter concert dates in Britain.

Propaganda was released in the US in January 1975 where it got to number sixty-three on *Billboard*'s Hot One Hundred chart. Having conquered the UK in 1974, Sparks' American *Propaganda* tour began in April 1975. The audiences lapped it up and as had been the case in the UK, prior to the start of the shows, pre-recorded Disney songs were played. After-show parties took place in America's Burger King restaurants. With ever the humorous and eccentric image maintained, Island Records got invites made; they stated, "black tie optional". It is strongly rumoured that the bootleg vinyl, *The Instant Darlings Recorded Live,* was recorded at this point in Sparks' career (the rumour is plausible based on the content of the recording). It is considered to be the very first Sparks bootleg but again, I am stating this with caution what with bootleg cataloguing (if any!) being such a grey area.

Representative of the scale of America's enthusiasm for Sparks, *Radio & Records* reported in June 1975: "Island recording group Sparks followed an Academy of Music stint in New York with a stopover at the local Burger King for a reception in their honour. The group successfully completed its first US tour and currently is preparing material for a new album to follow the current *Propaganda*."

Regarding Sparks' visit to the US not long prior to the

Left to right: Dinky Diamond, Trevor White, Ron Mael, Russell Mael and Ian Hampton.

interview, Russell was quoted in *Sounds* in September 1974: "Oh it was really incredible, well it was really a shock, the news had filtered about what was going on with the band in England so everyone in the States was aware of that. When we left Los Angeles we were just some local LA band who played the Whisky A Go Go. We went back and we're this regular band who, er, y'know, made it big in England. It was funny because we were treated differently than when we had lived there... it's just been amplified to like ten times of what it was before." Ron was quoted in the same feature: "All those countries look to England for their spiritual guidance." To which Russell was quoted: "They need to know what to be aware of then they pick up on it."

It's interesting to observe the ways in which the UK and the US had different points of reference when it came to how they engaged with new music. At least, that's how Sparks experienced such concept. Russell was quoted in the Texas paper, *The Marshall News Messenger*, in July 1975: "It's shocking to us to see that here in America people are concerned with the groups they grew up with — The Beatles and The Rolling Stones. The point of reference is still The Beatles. In England, we're the point of reference. It makes it exciting in England. You've got to keep on your toes. They want something fresh and new."

Propaganda was reviewed in *Cash Box* in January 1975: "Captured within its classic cover, Sparks generate another bout with the light-hearted approach to the heaviness of life via the rock medium. Ron Mael's insane lyricism, delivered with perfection by his vocalist brother, Russ Mael, and backed by a tighter-than-ever core of British musicians, makes this album a potential blockbuster. The pace of Sparks' music, intensely instrumental and involving rock hooks from every dusty corner imaginable, is breathtaking once you've adjusted your heartbeat to it. The lyrics command study and the music demands movement. Included is their recent British hit, 'Never Turn Your Back On Mother Earth'.

In a beautiful turn of events, having gone to the UK and risen to fame and success there in 1974, when back in America, Sparks were given a hero's welcome. They were featured in many popular US music magazines and made a range of TV appearances. They were on NBC's music show, *The Midnight Special*, and were also filmed at the Beacon Theatre in New York. Their performance was broadcast on *Don Kirschner's Rock Concert* and featured 'Something For The Girl With Everything', 'Talent Is An Asset' 'Hasta Mañana Monsieur', 'Thank God It's Not Christmas', 'B.C.' and 'Here In Heaven'. Sparks were also on ABC's *In Concert* where they were introduced by Keith Moon and Ringo Starr. Sparks also performed 'This Town Ain't Big Enough For Both Of Us' and 'B.C.' on *American Bandstand*. Russell was quoted of how American audiences were responding to Sparks in the *Newark Advocate* in July 1975: "People have been coming, on this tour, knowing our two latest LPs and shouting out. asking for songs. When we do 'This Town Ain't Big Enough For Both Of Us' they react exactly as if it's a big hit." By then, it was.

Chapter Six

1974 Was Just The Beginning

In September 1974, Sparks were voted as the "brightest new hope" in *Melody Maker*. Other acts at the top of their game (at least according to such polls) around this time were Queen, Slade, David Bowie, T. Rex and Mud. *Cash Box* reported in October 1974: "The brothers Mael and friends chose a captivating moment to line up for mug shots during the taping of a KMET Radio special presentation of Sparks, Island Record artists, live in concert. The group's arrival in Los Angeles coincided with *Melody Maker*'s announcement naming their single, 'This Town Ain't Big Enough For Both Of Us' best single of the year and the group 'Brightest Hope' (sic) and precedes the release of their newest American single, 'Talent Is An Asset.'"

It could be considered that commercially, 'This Town Ain't Big Enough For Both Of Us' was the making of Sparks. As Paul Morley (under the nom de plume of Gummo Mael) wrote of the track in the liner notes for the album released in 1990, *Mael Intuition:* "a startled, shiny/matt, smooth/rough, opaque/translucent, thick/thin, collision and bruise song, a crammed scam through the imagined Mael world of inzany pressure and emotional crack. It was a bit of heart beating shock to a tamed pop system, and shot them into the charts, just like that."

Russell was quoted in *The Irish News* in June 2018: "We were fortunate that we stumbled into things and they worked for us... We were really naïve and green at the time. You never really thought that this could be something we would still be doing and we'd have twenty-three albums and I'd be talking to you about this stuff today... We're proud things worked out in the right direction and we didn't have to rethink our life goals."

There's also a strong sense that 'This Town Ain't Big Enough For Both Of Us' and indeed *Kimono My House* were very much of their time. Ron was quoted in *Record Collector* in July 2003: "I could never see someone like Todd sign a band like us and release a record like that now. To sell the way it did and for a major label to continue with the band? It just wouldn't happen. There's not time for a band to develop, but the third album might be the one. It was in our case. I don't think people would have such patience with us today."

One of the many fascinating things about Sparks is that – even if there has been an element of being in the right place at the right time – when there hasn't been a strong commercial call for the type of music they wanted to make, they've made it anyway. Now of course, having Island behind them was probably a large help commercially but all the same it is to Sparks' credit that they have always done their own thing and (seemingly) not made their music with marketing in mind. Russell was quoted in *Sounds* in January 1975: "We always thought that we had commercial capabilities without adapting it to a standardised format. And we really had trouble convincing people."

That's powerful (and in a way, brave!); to command a place in the market when you're not even sure that what you're offering will be in demand. Russell was quoted in *Record Collector* in July 2003: "We don't think a band would get signed with a song like 'This Town Ain't Big Enough For Both Of Us'. People in labels want to know there's a market for what you are doing in some kind of way. There was little precedent or market for a song like that. We've been fortunate at times, sticking up for what you think is right – and at times it has worked – especially with *Kimono My House*." He was quoted in the same feature: "There was never a niche for us to comfortably rest in. We eventually created our own and everybody else came to it."

Russell was quoted in *The Times Magazine* in March 2003: "With Sparks we've never enjoyed the kind of commercial success which allows us to just sit back and watch life go by. So we did what we're capable of doing best – which is coming up with something that doesn't necessarily fit in, and then taking it to the extreme. Often when we fit least, is when the public like us most."

He was quoted in *Sounds* in January 1975: "The music's the most important end of it, and just so you're aware of what you're doing and don't start adapting what you're doing to the commercial type... You just have to use your own conscience. Think first of all what could appeal to you as opposed to what someone else wants to hear you do. You have to have a little blind faith in what you're doing and say I'm going to take a chance and try this and see what happens. I think as long as you can continue to excite yourself with what you're doing you'll be successful – we hope so anyway."

Disco 45 reported in June 1974:

Undoubtedly the most original record of 1974 so far (and it's likely to retain the title) is the amazing single by Sparks, 'This Town Ain't Big Enough For Both Of Us', which seems as if it will remain on everyone's lips for quite a while to come! So who are these people who can suddenly produce a record of such quality? The answer is in two parts. The first is composed of two brothers, Ron and Russell Mael. Ron is the piano player who never changes his expression and is the man responsible for writing the hit single and all but two tracks on the current Sparks album, *Kimono My House* (the other two he merely co-wrote with Russell). A prodigious talent, obviously as is Russell, who has a fascinatingly original voice, and is the group's vocalist, the good looker with the black curly hair.

They come from the land of great music, California, where they formed a group with three other guys from the University of California, Los Angeles, where they were studying. The group was called Halfnelson, and the members, apart from the Maels, were Earle Mankey, Jim Mankey and Harley Feinstein. It took a long time before Halfnelson were able to sufficiently interest a record company into giving them a recording contract. The company was Bearsville, an American label owned and managed by Albert Grossman, the manager of Bob Dylan – and the interest was actually shown by Todd Rundgren's girlfriend of the time (Todd is now a major star in his own right, of course) and Todd was chosen to produce the first album, which was released in 1972.

The record didn't sell so the group changed their name to Sparks and re-released the record under their new name, this time getting into the American top one hundred with a single called 'Wonder Girl'.

Shortly afterwards, the group came to Europe and appeared on *The Old Grey Whistle Test*, attracting a good deal of attention, and making the success of their second album, *A Woofer In Tweeter's Clothing*, seem assured. Despite all the best laid plans, the record was not terribly successful and Sparks split up because of lack of success. Fortunately for us, the man who had managed Sparks during their European tour was enormously excited by Ron and Russell and it was this man, John Hewlett, who is now the group's manager, who convinced Island's then A and R manager Muff Winwood, that the Mael brothers were not in any way ordinary talents. Thanks Muff!

All publicity is good publicity though, right? Russell was quoted in *Record Collector* in July 2003: "We were sent over in 1972 by Bearsville. They shipped us here (UK) to make a go of it. It was great. We had a residence at The Marquee and we got on *The Old Grey Whistle Test*... That one show did wonders for us. There was a bit of excitement and that's what ultimately generated the interest that led us to Island Records." (Sparks played on the 21st November 1972 broadcast of the show — the same one that featured Bill Withers' performance of "Ain't No Sunshine").

Ron was quoted of Todd Rundgren in *Record Collector* in July 2003: "He encouraged us to be as eccentric as we could be musically and he pushed us to be better, but he wasn't altering what we were doing." To which Russell was quoted: "We later realised that not all record producers do that. A and R people then get involved. There is no reason for A and R people to exist — people that are paid to take what you have and smooth down the rough edge and get rid of any character that may be involved to make it palatable. We were so spoiled working with Todd, we didn't know what a producer does."

Russell was quoted in *The Guardian* in August 2017: "It was a dream of ours to come to the UK in the seventies and be given a record deal with Island Records, as we were huge Anglophiles. It was a huge culture shock to come here, we were from LA and used to sunny skies every day, but the music scene and the opportunity for us to record an album which became *Kimono My House* was such an amazing opportunity for us, that the culture shock aside, we were just really happy... Even before we came here (the UK), just reading Sherlock Holmes, that was our view of what England was — this kind of fuzzy, brick buildings, vaguely mysterious... that whole sort of thing. We'd never been here, so it was like a fantasy place for us, both musically and in a more general way."

Being with Island Records in 1974 seems like it was generally a positive source of inspiration for the Maels. Ron was quoted in *Loud And Quiet* in July 2018: "I hate to hark back but when we were on Island Records in the seventies and you had groups like Roxy Music, you would hear them and you would feel kind of threatened but it would be a good type of threatened. You'd realise it was good stuff, so you'd have that feeling of wanting to surpass somebody else. We find less of that now."

Ron was quoted in *Diffuser* in September 2017: "In the seventies, we liked when we were kind of label rivals with

Roxy Music where they would come out with something, then we would come out with something. We always felt an unspoken rivalry that was a pushing rivalry that made for better music."

Sparks had come such a long way in such a short space of time and ultimately, the events of 1974 were a key part of the journey. It was surmised in the *Newcastle Evening Chronicle* in October 1975:

> The Maels come from Los Angeles (where the Hitler looks of Ron would cause less comment perhaps, than they would in downtown Newcastle, if there is such a place as downtown Newcastle) and they touted round for years a band which rejoiced under the name of Halfnelson. The sort of gig that the Maels then played was the high schools and, would you believe, church halls. The money came in, but the recording contracts didn't.

> Then on to the scene came the archetype Philadelphia whiz-kid, Todd Rundgren, who had produced bands like Bad Finger, Fanny, Grand Funk Railroad and The Band. Pretty soon the Halfnelson tag was dropped and Sparks arrived. Why? The reply I got from the publicists of the group was rather tongue in cheek: 'for no reason than it was inoffensive, boring but had connotations which sounded like a rock band and helped US journalists to think up headlines like Bright Sparks, Sparks Will Fly, Hot Sparks and Sparks Sparkle ad infinitum.'

> The band progressed from local dates to the coast to coast ones, and then in October 1972

they arrived in Britain at the start of a three-month European tour. Then, early in 1973, Ron and Russell contacted Island, who asked the group to fly to London to cut some demo tapes. The company decided that the songs were there but that the band itself needed radical rethinking. Dinky Diamond was found playing old Sparks material in a London club and was also found to be enough of a ham to fit in with the group's odd approach to visual humour. Martin Gordon and Adrian Fisher, bass and guitar, were found, conventionally enough, by ads in the trade papers.

With the band together, the first album was a natural progression. It came out as *Kimono My House* and the single, of course, was 'This Town Ain't Big Enough For Both Of Us', which was something of a revolution in music. It reached number three and before a British tour, Martin Gordon dropped out of Sparks to be replaced by Ian Hampton and Trevor White was added on second guitar. Both Hampton and White were in a band called Jook, a little-known outfit whose records and image were always ahead of their time and whose records, incidentally, are now something of collectors' items.

Adrian Fisher left the band after the fourth album, *Propaganda*, but not before a tour which featured hordes of people involved in an "Adolf Hitler lookalike contest" at every gig, and a delighted Russell having his trousers ripped off. Such is fame.

Two singles that got into the charts were culled from *Propaganda* and then the band went on their first real American tour.

Sparks recorded an acoustic version of 'This Town Ain't Big Enough For Both Of Us' in 1985. It was used as the B-side for their single, 'Change', a track from the 1986 album, *Music That You Can Dance To* ('Change' is substituted for the track, 'Armies Of The Night' on Non-US versions of the album).

In 1997 on their *Plagiarism* album, Sparks performed a new version of 'Amateur Hour' with Erasure. Some songs from *Propaganda* were also remade for the *Plagiarism* album. The acapella 'Propaganda' includes the verses that were omitted from the original album. On the remake of 'Something For The Girl With Everything', Tony Visconti orchestrated the strings. 'Never Turn Your Back On Mother Earth' included an orchestra and choir. With the track being almost ballad-like, it is understandable as to why it has had such mileage over the years. The song has been covered by a number of artists: Depeche Mode (in 1987 for a fan club flexi-disc), Martin Gore (in 1989 on his first solo album), Billy McKenzie (the song was released posthumously in 2005 – Billy died in 1997) and Neko Case (in 2009).

Sparks were actually reluctant to make the *Plagiarism* album. Russell was quoted in *Record Collector* July 2003: "We were really opposed to the idea of doing that album, as we'd opened up this whole new audience, especially in Germany. It was suggested to bring these people up to speed. Although we were initially ambivalent, we were excited to be working with Tony Visconti again. But we were never comfortable with the general direction."

As a band who has always been keen to move forward with their music, their perspective is understandable but on the other hand, the legacy of a fantastic discography is there so why not give it a new lease of life for a new audience? *Kimono My House* and *Propaganda* are two great Sparks albums, as their commercial success in 1974 illustrated; so musically, the mileage was there for development of such ideas and hence the *Plagiarism* album.

In terms of Sparks' overall history, *Propaganda* is a big deal because it was their second highest charting album for forty-three years, prior to the release of *Hippopotamus* in 2017. Equally, *Propaganda* remains as Sparks' highest charting album in the US.

Kimono My House features elements of glam rock and pop and even some baroque influences (as is evident in some of the chord patterns on the track 'Here In Heaven'). There are also some subtle baroque influences on the track, 'At Home, At Work, At Play' (particularly the section beginning with the lyrics, "You gotta catch her while...") on *Propaganda*.

During the recording sessions for *Indiscreet*, Sparks' 1975 album that followed *Propaganda*, a version of 'Never Turn Your Back On Mother Earth' was recorded by Tony Visconti's then wife, Mary Hopkin. It wasn't until 2007 however, that her version of the song was officially released. It features on her retrospective album, *Valentine*.

Released almost a year after *Propaganda*, *Indiscreet* came out in October 1975. Commercially, it didn't do as well as *Kimono My House* or *Propaganda*. *Indiscreet* got to number eighteen in the UK and to number one hundred and sixty-nine in the US. From the album, 'Get In The Swing' and 'Looks, Looks, Looks' were released as singles. In the UK singles chart, they reached numbers twenty-seven and twenty-six respectively. *Indiscreet* took a new direction really. Muff Winwood was no longer Sparks' producer. Of course, Tony Visconti still brought something positive to the proceedings, so much so that the Maels would work with him a good few decades later in their career. Also, from the *Indiscreet* album, the track, 'How Are You Getting Home?' was used in Leos Carax's (2012) film, *Holy Motors*.

When the Mael brothers elected to work with Tony Visconti on *Indiscreet*, he was already known for his work with David Bowie and Marc Bolan. Russell was quoted in *Get Ready To Rock* in December 2007: "I think that was more a musical and taste kind of decision than anything, 'cos we loved Tony intensely as a real musician and as an engineer and producer. So the decision was more about the fact that he could do those big band arrangements and could arrange outside instruments like he did on tracks like 'Looks, Looks, Looks', 'Get In The Swing', 'It Ain't 1918' etc. So it was those elements that drew us to Tony and not the fact he had a recording connection with the glam scene."

Even by 1975 after the release of their *Indiscreet* album, a considerable extent of Sparks' live set consisted of material from *Kimono My House* and *Propaganda*. It was reported in the *Acton Gazette* on 30th October 1975:

> The sign outside the Hammersmith Odeon on Sunday evening said, "Sparks Are Flying Tonight". And they certainly were, although the atmosphere was bright and happy as opposed to the heavy fanaticism shown at the Black Sabbath show.
>
> Only eighteen months ago, Sparks were being universally hailed as the band most likely to lift the music world from a pit of deep recession. Now, with a string of hit singles and best-selling albums to their credit, response from the critics has become rather less ecstatic, although Sparks

remain one of the most original bands in the business. They got things moving right away by opening the set with 'Get In The Swing' and followed it up quickly with 'B.C.', a favourite from the *Propaganda* album.

The Mael brothers were in fine form: Russell strutting and flapping about, dressed in a suit, the trousers neatly tucked into his knee-length boots, with a shirt, a striped tie and a pair of braces. Ron in the familiar ill-fitting white shirt, tie and baggy trousers, his head inclined at an impossible angle, giving his death's head glare into space.

Live, Sparks are just as precise as on record, despite the intricate arrangements and sudden rhythm changes. Dinky Diamond on drums and Ian Hampton on bass were spot on every time, providing a faultless platform for Trevor White's guitar licks and Ron Mael's jabbing piano chords. On top of it was the incomparable voice of Russell Mael, one-minute low and manly, the next, soaring into one of those eccentric falsetto vocal runs. From their new album, *Indiscreet*, they played 'Without Using Hands', 'Hospitality On Parade', 'It Ain't 1819' and 'In The Future'. They also included a number of old favourites like 'Talent Is An Asset' and 'Falling In Love With Myself Again' (from *Kimono My House*) and 'Achoo' from *Propaganda*. Of course, the set was sprinkled with well known Sparks hits — 'This Town Ain't Big Enough For Both Of Us', 'Amateur Hour', 'Never Turn Your Back On Mother Earth', 'Something For

The Girl With Everything' and 'Get In The Swing'. For an encore, they played 'Looks, Looks, Looks' and 'How Are You Getting Home?' from *Indiscreet*. One girl got quite carried away. She made it on to the stage and almost succeeded in grabbing Ron who kept on staring, unperturbed. Her second run on to the stage was more successful – she managed to hold on to Russell for a few precious seconds before being unceremoniously bundled back into the audience.

Indiscreet was reviewed in the *Hammersmith & Shepherd's Bush Gazette* in October 1975:

After having been heralded as the saviours of pop music and the innovators of an exciting, genuinely original sound, Sparks seem to have fallen a little by the wayside. They have, in short, failed to live up to the glowing reputation that was foisted on them by ecstatic music critics and which they never really warranted in the first place.

The power of Sparks' popularity lies in three very definite areas – the strange vocal abilities of Russell Mael, the even stranger visual appearance of his brother Ron, and the very complicated, yet highly polished arrangements of their songs. Credit for the production on this latest album lies at the doorstep of Tony Visconti, but ever since their beginning with 'This Town Ain't Big Enough For Both Of Us', I have felt the intricacies of Sparks' music have wrongly been put before the actual tunes. This album may be full of clever musical twists and turns and sound very glossy and chic, but even after listening to it several times there were very few actual tunes that stuck in my mind. They were all lost in one long blur of double tracked vocals, speeded up guitars and bizarre orchestrations.

Russell Mael's voice doesn't help this stilted feeling about their music – he sounds something like a cross between Bryan Ferry and Marc Bolan with his very unnatural and half talked, half sung vocals. It's true this album is at least different from the run of the mill pop record but whether that's because Sparks have any more talent than the others, or because they've just gone out of their way to be strange is a matter for debate.

Essentially, after the immense success of *Kimono My House* and *Propaganda*, Sparks had set the bar immensely high, both commercially and musically. It was probably inevitable that at some point, any album that was to follow their work in 1974 would be put under some extent of scrutiny. It just so happened that the album in the firing line was *Indiscreet*. Give it a listen and make up your own mind really. Ron was quoted in *Record Collector* in July 2003: "We took pride in things like 'Get In The Swing', things our new audience would enjoy while we were trying out new ideas musically."

It was rumoured in *Cash Box* in January 1976: "Russ and Ron Mael have apparently abandoned the vehicle known as Sparks in their bid for stardom. The question is, without the Maels can one even consider the remainder a continuing band? Anyway, The Mael Brothers is probably the nom de musique being adopted." Sparks' long-term discography makes it clear that this was definitely a rumour. Maybe the media were missing their Sparks fix for a brief period while the Maels were busy working on their next album. We'll never know but it's good that it was just a rumour. Well, I say rumour but it's a question of semantics really and who/which line-up is referred to as a means of defining the Sparks name. It was considered in the *Reading Evening Post* in November 1986: "They always put out quirky and witty but very strong songs but just when hits like 'This Town Ain't Big Enough For Both Of Us', 'Looks, Looks, Looks' and 'Amateur Hour' seemed set to make them comfortable chart stars, they split up."

Ron and Russell didn't split as a duo. That has emerged to be ongoing over the years. Ron was quoted in *The Times Magazine* in March 2003: "We don't do a lot of things other than music together, but I definitely think that if we weren't brothers we wouldn't have lasted so long. Even though we don't tend to have similar likes and dislikes as regards to music outside of Sparks, within Sparks we really do have a very definite idea of what we like and don't like."

After their tour of the US in 1975, Ron and Russell decided that they would no longer be working with the UK nucleus of Sparks. With the UK members of the group no longer part of a band, their initial plan was to keep going. Ian Hampton, Trevor White and Dinky Diamond, with Adrian Fisher back in the fold, rehearsed some material over the course of a week at Island Studios in London. Four songs were recorded during such time. Ian, Trevor and Dinky all contributed vocals on the project. Upon being presented with the tape, Island Records made the decision not to take the project any further. I advocate that there is a great sadness about this on account of the fact that all four artists concerned were a big part of Sparks' achievements in 1974.

It's a real shame to think that really, in their rejection of this project, Island were pretty much sending out a message of "we're behind the Mael brothers but we're not behind you." Ouch! That said, as much as Island were growing as a company by that time, they weren't the be all and end all of the music industry so it may have been the case that approaching other record companies may have gone in favour of Hampton, Diamond, White and Fisher. Based on what the musicians contributed to Sparks in 1974, it is plausible that they may have had mileage as a band in their own right, without the Mael brothers at the forefront.

By 1975, Ron and Russell were in demand to the extent that other high-profile artists were keen to work with them. As well as the Jacques Tati project that sadly fell through, in November 1975, the *Daily Mirror* reported: "Nine years after her first record, Marianne Faithful is bursting into song again. The twenty-eight-year-old blonde has released a disc called 'Dreamin' My Dreams' and is already planning the follow up – with Sparks. Ron Mael of Sparks has written a song for Marianne to record with his brother, Russell. She is flying to New York to record the song called 'Room For Two' later this month." The reasons aren't clear but the project didn't go ahead.

Russell was quoted in *Sounds* in January 1975: "There's a lot of offers in different areas but we really don't want to cheat Sparks, we don't want to let it suffer in any way. I'd like to take part in films that are totally divorced from rock or pop music, I'd rather do a dramatic role and I'd really like to do that. I'm sure I will be doing it. I just don't want to be involved in a version of *A Hard Day's Night.*"

It was reported in *The Times Magazine* in March 2003: "Sparks have grown up and endured while being surrounded by myths and suppositions. Their image seemed to prompt a widely held belief that the brothers lived together in a kind of 'Sparks House', pursuing an ascetic and asexual existence with the disciplinary routine of a couple of philosopher scientists. And while they did live together for a while in London during the seventies (in a flat beneath that of the theatre critic Kenneth Tynan), the facts of their lifestyle are somewhat less dramatic. Sparks have enjoyed constant levels of commercial and critical success which allows them to concentrate on making music and touring."

Overall, the Mael brothers have managed to maintain a fascinating dynamic with the media. Ron and Russell were asked very explicitly by the interviewer in *Beat Instrumental* in August 1974, "Do you come from rich parents?" to which Ron was quoted: "Fairly well off, yeah." Another very targeted question in the same interview was "Do you have a social conscience?" Ron was quoted: "I used to have one actually. I used to do things like in Los Angeles there's the Watts area and I gave musical instruction there for a while, taught the guitar actually. After a while I started to ask myself those sort of questions, like is this really helping them or am I doing it to ease my own conscience? And then I got really busy and I didn't have the time to do it and then I realised that it was obviously just helping me. So I don't know what the real answer is."

And so the interviewer asked: "So you're going to make it on your own terms and the wider questions like poverty don't bother you too much?" Russell; "Well right now we're so engrossed in what we're doing, our vision is just like a tunnel and I think that's how it should be at the moment. We want to do what we're doing more than anything else. This will sound conceited, but what we're doing wouldn't be as good as it is if we were concerned with other things right now. I mean, if we could see what we're doing from another angle, it wouldn't be the same. For us this is no steppingstone. What we're doing now is it."

I can't be the only one who thinks that the interviewer's questions here were at least a little crass. Every successful musician could be asked the same questions and yet it comes across that the interviewer was possibly asking Ron and Russell to justify their success because they are from a comfortable background. It's not how I would have chosen to conduct the interview if it were me in the interviewer's shoes but still, the feature overall shows that even in the early days of their fame, Ron and Russell were competent at interviews, even in instances where the questions were perhaps on the heavier side of things.

Still though, it could just have been the case that the interviewer was particularly skilled and interested in getting a dialogue going that went beyond the obvious stuff. The interview in *Beat Instrumental* in August 1974 got fascinatingly philosophical in parts. The interviewer asked the brothers: "I suppose that most of us are seeking happiness, do you really believe that success in this business will bring you that." Ron was quoted: "Well, first of all I would contest the idea that a person's aim is really happiness. I don't believe that such a thing as happiness is a state that lasts for a long time. I think there's individual moments of happiness, like having a bite of apple crumble makes me really happy, but I don't think that happiness can be maintained long. Personally, I don't want to feel contented, because I reckon I'd be in trouble if that happened. Then I would just be a contented vegetable. I'm just fascinated with the thing of energy and excitement and it seems that achieving a contented state is not what I'm looking for. I think that anyone who's really contented is half dead."

Russell was quoted: "I can be content with small things.

I mean, you can be content because you have a good house but then when you're in your good house you start shooting for something else. You have to have some drive. I think the drive is the end in itself. If you buy a good house, you get it because you'll have a better environment from which to work for something else."

That's some beautifully deep stuff there. Plenty of mind food miles outside of the music. In response, the interviewer asked, "Surely the moment you realise that the drive is an end in itself and not a means, you cancel out the need for the drive?" Ron was quoted: "All the time you're driving you're getting a feedback along the way. As you come across something new you're getting charged up and that's what pushes you along. You don't have a choice of continuing or not continuing, you just get carried away with it." A much better interview than asking a band what their favourite colour is! In the case of Sparks, it's an especially good interview considering how open they are overall.

Russell was quoted in *The Quietus* in August 2017: "We don't like talking about ourselves; I mean we've done it with you here for an hour, but we like to let the music be the spokesperson for us. So doing a memoir and all that chronological 'and then this happened and then blah blah' doesn't appeal to us that much. We think there's more mystique in what you don't know about. We've been approached about doing several documentaries and nobody can understand why we're resistant. We want an angle or approach that would be fitting to our sensibility rather than just a dry talking-heads-style documentary."

In interviews where the Mael brothers got talking more about their likes and dislikes and general interests, comedy and food were often the subjects of choice. In July 1974 when *Melody Maker* featured small biographies of the Sparks line-up who were on the *Kimono My House* tour (Trevor White, Ian Hampton, Adrian Fisher, Dinky Diamond and the Maels), whilst the rest of the band's biographies were pretty standard, what was written about Ron and Russell was more conversational.

The feature said of Russell:

Russell, explaining the new gourmet way of eating a long lunch. What he and Ron do, he says, is to eat a selection of starters, leave the main course and then eat a selection of the desserts. That way he gets to "eat a lot of the desserts which are, after all, the best part of the meal". Thus after eating immeasurable types of starters (pâté, sea food salad, various soups, trout, melon, Italian hors d'oeuvres) the brothers Mael bounded on to such delicacies as zabaglione, apple pie, mozzarella and other cheeses, lemon and orange sorbets until finally the chef sent down a white flag and the premises were vacated.

Now the tour of Britain's restaurants (taking in the odd, frantic gig) has been completed, Sparks are going in the studios to record the next album. Russell has "one of my gems in the six-month plan, so that'll be there and in the three days maybe another one'll come out and maybe not", he sniffs. The tour: "It's been amazing. We didn't know what to expect at all. We've never gotten reactions like what we've gotten. We've been doing what we've been doing for a while and it's a bit disorientating for a while to have people liking what you're doing after sort of mildly accepting you in the past — very mildly —

to sort of finding them liking you in abundance. You kinda go 'what?! They're cheering for us?' It's really a strange feeling. It's a good feeling."

They still haven't figured out why it should have happened so suddenly beyond "the time is right" and one feels they're not particularly concerned with analytical intellectualising. They're just accepting it and that's the way it should be ("It was still a bit of a Sparks Free Trial Offer Tour in that everybody was still feeling their way and nobody knew what the reaction was going to be and no-one knew if anybody would show up to some of the gigs but they sure did. It was a learning process for everybody. For The Real Tour that happens in November").

On stage Sparks use lights to good, simple effect. Two bright, white spots pick out Ron and Russell throughout, a little like the convict captured in the copper's torch beam ("We had discussed it with the lighting crew and said that we wanted it to be featuring us in a way that wasn't overtly theatrical, but would present us really well as just our personalities. We wanted to create the atmosphere. We wanted to *be* the atmosphere and we did it I think by using just those spots 'cos we're really concerned that we didn't want to get into elaborate presentations and outdoing everybody with elaborate Busby Berkeley choreographed settings and all that stuff. People have said that our music is really theatrical at times but if it is at all we wanted it to come from the songs having a theatrical tinge to them, if they do, and from our personalities. Rather than combining rock and theatre. I dunno, it's better to go see the Royal Shakespeare Company than see a rock band trying to be theatrical").

The Maels and humour go very much hand in hand. When they're together and able to spot situations and targets for their barbs it can be an exhibition of the driest American wise-cracking. What sort of English humour appeals to them? "It's a cliché but we might have to say the *Monty Python* thing. Just that sort of mentality seems to be on our wavelength as opposed to the bingo hall mentality where they're appealing to ladies that just got home from the bingo club. What's the guy, the *Amateur Hour* guy? Hughie Green, that type of thing and a lot of the serials that are 'funny' about the working class English where he comes now and says 'I'm feeling pretty randy' and everybody goes 'ha-ha-ha-ha', just the common denominator sort of humour. It gives me the same feeling as when we're driving along past the bingo halls and you see the old ladies queuing up. I find that really depressing."

And of Ron:

Old Stoneface sat there and looked like he was gonna explode. It was just after midnight and Sparks had just played a far from satisfactory gig in Cambridge's Corn Exchange, which does a fair imitation of a derelict railway shed. All he wants now is peace and quiet but this girl journalist is asking him the most idiotic questions. He's tried using his tinder-dry US humour on her but she doesn't seem to dig. So he turns round and snaps, "Look, I'm gonna have this girl thrown out. John will you throw her out?"

He doesn't of course. Far too polite for that. So the wise-cracks continue, raining down like arrows on Custer. That is one chink in Ron Mael's armour. He cannot tolerate fools and will not have his time wasted by them. But now Ron will be off on the road and ready to start work on the next Sparks album. "It's mostly all written," he says, "we have three days to do some more writing and augment what's been done. It's hard to describe what it is other than that a similarity is that it will still be songs as opposed to uh, long tracks." Once again, most of the songs will be Ron's.

The tour, which ended at the Rainbow, Finsbury Park, last Sunday had been set up well before the single became a hit so the gigs tended to be a little out of the ordinary. Both Ron and Russell have a history of creative work outside music which may continue at some time but wouldn't be combined in rock, says Ron. Music is their main preoccupation. "I see our songs", says Ron, "as dramatic only in the way that the arrangements and moods shift, but not dramatic in a stagey way. It's a less obvious sort of drama. It isn't exactly demonstrating what's happening in a plot. The song itself is the drama and the people within

the band performing those songs are so close
and part of the song that, in a way, they're actors
in that drama. But not 'actor' actors. You can't even
separate the players from the song."

Sparks' music is a heady mixture of clever lyrics,
in live performance often losing point and
subtlety beneath the band's instrumental power
as Russell tussles with the helter-skelter melody
line and navigates arrangements highlighted by
sudden pauses. There's one moment in the show
when the one show tune, 'Wonder girl', Sparks' old
US hit single, fades to a whisper with Russell on
the far side of the stage in a gradually dimming
spot. Then, startlingly, Ron's intro to 'This Town'
rings out and a bright, white spot picks him up
on the opposite side of the stage to brother Russ.
That kills me every time ("Yeah, that kills me
too, that's really bright. Stabs right into my eyes
there").

Of the difference between English and American
humour? "I really think I can understand English
humour but people mention certain types
of English humour to us that we really find
ridiculous. But there are exact equivalents of that
English humour in American humour." In English
humour, they say, they laugh at *Monty Python* and
such like, never probably having the opportunity
to see the likes of early Tony Hancock. What about
US funnies?: "Well", says Ron, pursing his lips and
pressing finger tips together like a judge about
to sum up, "I think we're really gonna contradict

ourselves here 'cos I really like Abbott and
Costello, *Sergeant Bilko* and Laurel and Hardy"
and, they add, the original *I Love Lucy* with good
ol' Fred and Ethel Mertz living downstairs ("Hmm.
I think we've dug ourselves a little grave there'").

Stoneface indeed! There was definitely, for want of better term perhaps, method in the madness. Ron was quoted in *Classic Pop* in March 2015: "The singer is always the flashy and sexy guy, so it's about making the obvious contrast. In my experience, it's hard for a keyboard player to be flashy in the way a guitarist is without looking ludicrous. The way to go is in the opposite direction and be immobile, so that it comes across as an intentional artistic move, when really it's made out of necessity. It distils the whole band to its barest parts." Upon being asked, "What are you thinking about when you're giving the patented Ron Mael 'death stare' on stage?", Ron was quoted in the same feature: "I'm just concentrating! I was aware when Sparks started doing *Top Of The Pops* that there were a lot of close-ups. Rather than look distracted, I took it to the extreme as a way to focus on what I'm doing, not just look like I'm vaguely wandering through a song. Some people look good smiling, some don't – and I'm in the latter camp. A slight scowl is more my style than an amiable grin."

Ron was quoted of his famous glare in *New Musical Express* in November 1974: "Oh, it's not something I practice. In a way, it helps to cut one off, though of course, I'm conscious of what's going on, especially when it comes to my part. I was never a great mover, lousy at all dances and all, that's Russell's department."

Upon being asked, "Where did (your) infamous piano bench smashing come from? Was this a product of The Who or a weird rebellion for keyboard players?", Ron was quoted in *Northern Transmissions* in 2018: "When we first started, we always admired the British bands much more than the American bands. Especially The Who and The Kinks, but I always wanted to be Pete Townshend but when you're a keyboard player there's not a lot of possibilities outside of writing to be him. I went the other direction since I was tied down to the bench, and I didn't want to be an animated keyboardist, instead I wanted to be Pete so that's where that probably came from."

It was between 16th May and 11th June 2008 that Sparks performed (at the time) all twenty-one of their albums at the Islington Academy in London. The shows climaxed into the live debut of their twenty-second album, *Exotic Creatures Of The Deep*. With regards to the twenty-one albums in twenty-one nights in 2008, Russell was quoted in *Diffuser* in September 2017: "Our manager came up with that. It was one of those things, great conceptual thing. We're always for big concepts, then the reality was trying to figure out, after we came back down from the euphoria of 'this is a fantastic idea', was to figure out how we're going to logistically do it, to learn that many songs. It was a big challenge and it was something that no one else could do and probably no one else will ever do cause it's pretty labour intensive. First of all it requires you to have that many albums before you can consider to do something similar. Most of the bands who have twenty-one albums that I'm aware of would be too lazy to attempt this."

Russell was quoted in *SSG Music* in April 2013: "It was an event for us that no one else will ever do. For a few reasons. There are not many bands that have as big a catalogue for starters and the ones that do, they become lazy and don't have the drive or stamina to want to undertake something like that, because it took four months of rehearsing to be able to learn over two hundred and fifty songs with a group that was willing to stick with us and go along with our folly. It is a combination of things and I think that no one else will ever do something to that extent. It's a lot of work and you really have to be driven. The groups that do have that many albums, I can almost guarantee that they do not have the hunger, the need to do it. Then it is not so much a matter or being lazy. They do not need to prove a point in the same kind of way and really no one else will ever do anything like it... It was something both for ourselves and Sparks fans. It was a special thing, to put our whole catalogue into perspective and revisit songs, the majority of which we have never done live before, and to see all the albums we have done up to that point. For our fans as well, to hear everything we have ever done. There were quite a few people that came to the whole month of shows and we really have to hand it to them. People have lives and jobs, you know? Obligations, and to devote a month of your life to Sparks made us feel really good."

Propaganda was probably a difficult album to perform from a technical musicianship perspective. The speed of some of the songs is such that the scope to recover from mistakes would have been minimal. Still though, the performance was a success. With four decades of successful musicianship behind them, it's not surprising of Sparks really. Besides, the "Propaganda"/ 'At Home, At Work, At Play' segue was rehearsed extensively on the afternoon of the concert in order to ensure that it would be perfect, live in the evening. Ron did his comic shuffle dance during 'Who Don't Like Kids' and promised not to do it again. A broken promise and rightly so! 'Lost And Found' was played as the encore.

The way in which *Kimono My House* and *Propaganda* brought Sparks to the attention of the public is such that over the years, there has been interest in their earlier discography. Upon being asked how he felt about *Kimono My House* decades after it was made and whether he wished he had done anything different on the album, Russell was quoted in *SSG Music* in April 2013: "I do not think so... We are really happy with our career."

With regards to *Propaganda* and where it sits as part of Sparks' history, Russell was quoted in the same feature: "We always feel that we want to be pushing things forward for ourselves and our fans. First always has to be for ourselves. We feel like we are constantly trying to do something that is bucking the system."

Since 1973, Sparks' second album on Bearsville has been re-released several times along with the band's first album. One such release came out in 1975 in direct response to the success of Sparks in 1974. Essentially, through the band having raised their profile via *Kimono My House* and *Propaganda* on Island, there was scope to capitalise on their back catalogue, which people were now more interested in than when such albums were released. The 1975 release of Sparks' Bearsville albums was packaged as two LPs in a gatefold sleeve and a fourteen-page booklet was included. In 1988, *A Woofer In Tweeter's Clothing* was first released on CD. The artwork on the original LP release of *A Woofer In Tweeter's Clothing* was photographed by Larry DuPont and Ron Mael.

Russell was quoted in *Sounds* in January 1975: "I actually started writing before he got interested in writing songs and on the first (Bearsville) LP there were more of my songs on it and eventually Ron started getting involved in it... He wasn't writing on piano at that time, it was mostly on guitar and now he writes mostly on piano and I think that has changed the style of the songs. It's not that I've stopped writing but Ron's more prolific. He's been coming up with things that I've liked better." Whilst Russell contributed to the writing on *A Woofer In Tweeter's Clothing*, Ron was pretty much the main writer for the band thereafter.

Russell was quoted on the matter in *Get Ready To Rock* in December 2007: "I wrote some of it yeah, but not most of it. Yeah I contributed to it and did my fair share of the lyrics. And it is correct to say that the starting point for most of Sparks' songs is Ron's lyrics. He keeps pushing me to do more but I think Ron's stuff is better and besides, writing involves so much more work."

Several re-mastered editions of *Kimono My House* and *Propaganda* have been released (see the back of this book for details and track listings). Such was the importance on impact of Sparks' music in 1974. A re-mastered fortieth anniversary edition of *Kimono My House* was released in December 2014. It was in the same month that Sparks performed the entire album with the thirty-five piece Heritage Orchestra at the Barbican Centre. Nathan Kelly was responsible for the orchestral arrangements and the programme included songs from other albums in Sparks' discography. On account of the fact that the show sold out so quickly, a second date was soon added.

It was reported in the *Los Angeles Times* in February 2015:

> A little more than forty years ago, forward-looking LA rock band Sparks released their third album, *Kimono My House*, a work that influenced a lot of glam-rock, dance and electronic music that followed. This weekend, founding members

Ron and Russell Mael will play their commercial breakthrough album live in its entirety in two shows at the Theatre at Ace Hotel downtown. The Mael siblings will be accompanied Saturday and Sunday by a thirty-eight piece orchestra, which also will be on board for other songs spanning Sparks' four decade-plus recording career, specially arranged for these shows.

It won't be the first time the Mael brothers have performed *Kimono* from beginning to end. They also did it seven years ago in London during a stint in which they performed all (at that time) twenty-one of their studio albums live over the course of twenty-one non-consecutive nights.

Russell was quoted in the same feature: "We wanted the concert's orchestral arrangements to not simply be strings sweetening and playing behind a rock band but rather we wanted to do challenging, modern, complex arrangements. Members of the thirty-eight piece Heritage Orchestra in London told us that this was an extremely difficult and challenging score for them to do."

The feature continued: "In place of the Heritage Orchestra and conductor Jules Buckley, who performed for the London shows, Sparks will be supported by a local orchestra being assembled by part-time LA Philharmonic arranger-conductor Suzie Katayama, who also has recorded and toured with artists such as Bjork, Eric Clapton, Sheryl Crow and Barbra Streisand." To which Russell was quoted: "Whereas during the twenty-one-nights concert of *Kimono My House* in London, where we wanted to do a very faithful band performance of the original album — as we attempted to do for all twenty-one albums of ours at that time — the concept for these performances is to broaden our musical palette while still attempting to retain all of the eccentricity and flavour of the original album. Ron and I have rehearsed for the shows for about three months, however, the rehearsal process is really unique to what we're used to doing as we obviously can't have a thirty-eight piece orchestra with us for months on end. So our arranger, Nathan Kelly, made audio mock-ups of the orchestra doing the arrangements for us so we could rehearse with just the two of us and a good playback system. The shock was sitting down in front of the real orchestra in London and hearing how wonderfully different the real musicians' performances were to our demos... We're excited to do *Kimono* in LA, especially in such an appropriate venue as the elegant Ace Theatre. Any venue established by Charlie Chaplin and Co. is the right venue for us."

Upon being asked, "Considering you've had such a shifting cult following over the years, how has it been seeing the crowds change?", Russell was quoted in *Northern Transmissions* in 2018: "Curiously enough with the big body of work, there's people that have come in midway, or even more recently so the makeup of the audience is pretty diverse. Of course there are also people who know all our music. We did that twenty-one nights event where we did one of our albums every night in London, that also showed the makeup of which fan would come to which album. Now over time we're finding the audience is coming with a knowledge of the entire catalogue, thanks to the Internet, especially fans who might not have been there in the beginning." Ron was quoted: "The Internet's made everything contemporary, even stuff that's far enough back in your discography to be forgotten is easy to find."

Regarding the fact that for their 2008 concerts, different albums may have attracted different extents of audience interest, Russell was quoted in *Get Ready To Rock* in December 2007: "Well the whole project is more than being about the specifics of who will attend on which particular night. It's really more a statement of playing every single song and playing every single note off every single album we've ever done. The idea behind it is to find a bold way to introduce our latest, yet-to-be-released album. We just thought about the best way to focus on the new album and thought this would be a unique way of doing it. It shows how strongly we feel about the new album. So, the specifics are secondary to the concept of the event as a whole, which is bigger than any one night. You know the idea of a celebration of our twenty-one albums was so compelling that we wanted to do it this way. We understand of course that not everybody would want to spend a month of their life with Sparks but the idea was so compelling that we just had to do it."

When asked whose idea the project was, Russell was quoted in the same feature: "Well it came from high consultation and board room meetings with the principals of Sparks and Sparks' manager. We needed to come up with fresh and new ideas of how you want to present yourself. And the next album is very important so we thought it was better to bring attention to it in a noteworthy way. By doing it this way people would be thinking about our next piece of work. The hard work on our part is to get it all together but we are up for the count."

Chapter Seven

A Band Of Many Talents

In 1975 the Mael brothers moved back home to California. Russell was quoted in *Sounds* in January 1975: "We've been in Britain for one and a half years and it's two totally different worlds being in England and Los Angeles. It will be good for a change to be back there. It will have a certain effect on the music, it will give it a certain freshness." However, Ron was quoted in *Sounds* in December 1974: "I don't think LA will influence us at all in a musical kind of way because the things we do are really within our own world and outside things don't really tend to influence us in an obvious kind of way."

Perhaps they just fancied a change of scenery. Russell was quoted in the *Daily Mirror* in July 1979: "I don't think we were turning our backs on England but it is physically more comfortable in Los Angeles. There are a lot of economic problems in England too. It seems a lot worse now than when we came here in 1974. People have become so complacent."

Towards the later half of the seventies, Sparks wanted

to keep things fresh and they went for more of a West Coast sound and ultimately achieved this with the albums *Big Beat* (1976) and *Introducing Sparks* (1977). With regards to *Big Beat*, Ron was quoted in *Record Collector* in July 2003: "We went back to the States. We thought in our own delusional way that we should make something that sounded more American. It was exactly the wrong time and the wrong producer. Rupert Holmes was a great producer... But while we were in the States we thought, let's be doing something American, and it didn't really work." And of *Introducing Sparks:* "There was no sense of an edge. The album was too polished. It was done in a big studio and it was too produced for us."

On balance though, even at the peak of their success in 1974, it comes across that the Maels were always open to expanding the scope of their music. Russell was quoted in *Sounds* in June 1974: "We feel that we've got all the technique that one should have but we're trying to go one step further. When one has all the technique, one should try to go beyond that. To be totally wrapped up in the rock field, I don't think is very fulfilling, because when people are too involved they are inbred in the rock field. I think if anyone is going to do anything with a bit more substance, it hasn't got to be wrapped up in the rock field." Russell was quoted in *Sounds* in January 1975: "I just really enjoy doing things that won't be so predictable."

Besides, it comes across that Sparks have made good choices in terms of working within the scope of what they are capable of. When asked how he felt about the prospect of writing extensively long scores of music, Ron was quoted in *Sounds* in December 1974: "Yeah, it would be fun to play around with. I really don't have the desire to do an extended piece because you have to have such a strong overlaying theme tune to really carry it off. That just seems to counter what rock themes are all about to make something so important that it takes two sides to develop it."

After *Indiscreet*, it wasn't really until 1979's *No. 1 In Heaven* that Sparks were back on the radar in terms of commercial success. Russell was quoted regarding the direction they decided to take with *No.1 In Heaven* in *LA Weekly* in November 1998: "We thought the combination of the vocal with a really cold electronic sound was amazing, and we were getting tired of our musical surroundings — not the songs, but the trappings of a band."

In 1978, the Mael brothers made a radical decision to change things dramatically; they ditched the band format and termed up with Giorgio Moroder (the mastermind behind Donna Summer's 'I Feel Love') to make the album, *No. 1 In Heaven*; in terms of instrumentation it relied entirely on synthesisers. The album is regarded by many as an important landmark in the development of electronic music. Russell was quoted in *Loud And Quiet* in July 2018: "There was a time when punk stuff was coming in, like the Sex Pistols and stuff, and we loved them but we did wonder about feeling relevant at that time. When we did the *No. 1 In Heaven* album, that was really not fitting in in any kind of way. You didn't really know how to fit into that kind of world. Although strangely we became friends with Steve Jones from the Sex Pistols and was surprised to learn he loved things like 'Beat The Clock' from that album. It was flattering to know they were listening to it. So I guess sometimes when you do feel out of place, maybe what you're doing actually isn't as out of place as you may think." I advocate that there's definitely a positive message there in terms of the merit of an artist doing what feels right for them and not following the crowd.

Such philosophy is something that has probably served Sparks well over the years. Russell was quoted in *Loud And Quiet* in July 2018: "One of the reasons we remain being vital, in our minds, is that we really don't care all that much about those industry shifts. In the end you have to do something really strong, musically. Those other things have an importance but at the end of the day you're an artist who is doing music and the distribution and digital versus whatever... it's kind of not that important for us as musicians. I think it's a distraction for people to be all up in arms about. There's downsides to the system now in terms of people not buying as much and people using Spotify, but in the end that stuff is less important than what you're doing creatively. It's a lot harder to do good music than it is to moan about how inequitable the system is."

Russell was quoted in *Get Ready To Rock* in December 2007: "Working with Georgio opened up new ideas for us. For one thing it showed we weren't tied to the guitar, bass and drum format and it showed you could work in other ways in a non-band context. Making that record also showed that you could use electronics and then after that you could go on to use electronics with guitars. So I think in terms of finding a new way to present our songs he really opened up things for us... It was critically tough at the time 'cos people thought it was puzzling for Sparks to be doing what they perceived to be disco. We saw it as an electronic album where the synths had replaced the aggression of guitars, and really that album was about the songs. The way it worked we'd come up with some ideas and Georgio would tell us which ones he thought would work or not. We didn't set out to make 'disco record' as such it was more to do with the style and maybe the instrumentation of the thing, and even how it was recorded."

Ron was quoted of *No. 1 In Heaven* in *Record Collector* in July 2003: "We thought we'd taken the band format as far as it could go. We'd worked with Tony Visconti and he'd done all these amazing orchestrations around the band on *Indiscreet* but it was now time to approach it in a completely different way. We had heard (Donna Summer's) 'I Feel Love' and we thought that there must be a way to apply that sort of sound and thinking to what we were doing."

Sparks changed many times thereafter though and returned to using a more traditional band line-up, as well as playing live with orchestras and dabbling in techno music with the 1994 album, *Gratuitous Sax & Senseless Violins*. The 2002 album *Lil' Beethoven* is in the style of classically influenced pop art (and even then, I'm not trying to categorise their music too specifically – it's too diverse to be put in a single category really!). *Lil' Beethoven* features complex orchestral arrangements, as is demonstrated on the opening track, 'The Rhythm Thief'.

Chris Blackwell was quoted of 'The Rhythm Thief' in *The Times Magazine* in March 2003: "To me, it sounds incredibly fresh and theatrical, almost like an original cast album for a theatrical production. Now if 'The Rhythm Thief' can be heard on the radio, it'll be a traffic-stopper. It's totally different to anything else. In 1974 at Island we had a number two hit record with them, and this is similarly innovative. I hadn't spoken to them for nearly twenty-eight years, and then someone said I ought to listen to *Lil' Beethoven*, and I realised it sounded like tomorrow's record, you know? I think that they will be recognised as the geniuses that they really are."

Russell was quoted in *The Guardian* in August 2017: "The Island albums really mean a lot to us; we have other periods that also had a huge significance to us as well, for various reasons. Certain songs have been really successful in France for instance, and a song like 'When Do I Get To Sing My Way' (from *Gratuitous Sax & Senseless Violins*) was huge in Germany, so they have a huge emotional significance to us, because of the time they were in a particular part of the world. There were albums that were less well known in Europe but big in the States, especially on the West Coast, and we did large concerts in the US as a result, so the significance of a particular album has different meanings for us depending on the time they were released and the part of the world where they attracted more attention. Hopefully with *Hippopotamus* we'll have it be successful everywhere in the world at the same time." There's a lot of love for Sparks in Europe. It was reported in *The Times Magazine* in March 2003: "Over the years, Sparks have maintained a position halfway between cult status and commercial acceptability. Their European fans are legendary in their fanaticism."

Constant creativity has been a key ingredient in Sparks' career. It has probably put them in an excellent position of being unafraid to try new ideas. Hence the range of musical genres that Sparks have embraced throughout their career. Ron was quoted in *The Guardian* in August 2017: "I've never really felt a creative block. I think there are times where you might have some trouble coming up with either a song or a direction, but if you keep working, that's the solution. I have faith you can get through any of those slightly slower periods by simply pressing on, and the answer will come at some point. Abandoning what you've done in the past is a more general way to avoid the block – working with Giorgio Moroder in electronics, or *Lil' Beethoven*, where we decided to use strings and repetitive vocals instead of drums and guitars. The most important thing though is to not sit there and mope about the fact you're having a creative block – it seems like it's trying to romanticise your problems in some way. We try to find a solution, no matter how difficult it is, or if it requires you re-evaluating your whole approach to doing anything."

Just think, Sparks' musical legacy – in terms of how long they have been going and in terms of how many genres they have covered over the years – is phenomenal. From a band struggling to get their commercial breakthrough in Los Angeles to having a long-term career as band with cult popularity on an international basis, 1974 was really the turning point for Sparks. Whilst all of their albums sound, overall, very different to *Kimono My House* and *Propaganda*, commercially, those were the two albums that started it all for Ron and Russell Mael.

Lyrically, Sparks have always been an interesting band. They haven't always been too vocal on what those lyrics mean in each of their songs but really, should they have to as in, does good art need to be explained to be enjoyed? Ron was quoted in *Sounds* in June 1974: "I just have a feeling about lyric sheets. When lyrics are included with albums, sometimes they become too much of a be-all and end-all in themselves. I am glad that they were included just because people ask what the lyrics are and there's no other way of getting around it."

Phonetically alone, both *Kimono My House* and *Propaganda* are fascinating albums and the way each syllable fits with the melody is a joy to behold. Sparks' music is fast, complex and fun; quite possibly like the minds of the creators behind such music. Russell was quoted in *Exposed* in August 2017: "Ron is our chief lyricist and we have always had a real pride in special lyrics and that is always a challenge. We are trying to express ourselves in ways that are not tried and true. With pop music, we are trying to do that: to be abrasive. But abrasiveness does not have to be political. It is hard to describe what it is and it is hard not to be boring. The worst reaction is for the audience to be blasé about it and to not have any reaction at all."

Sparks' music has been a strong influence for many other artists. In particular, what Sparks did in 1974 has been applauded by a number of high-profile musicians whose careers began years afterwards. Bjork was quoted of hearing *Kimono My House* when she was eight in *Melody Maker* in July 1993: "(Sparks) were the most refreshing thing in my life." She was also quoted in *Q Magazine* in October 1993: "I loved the way Russell Mael sung like a geisha, and that they were into wearing geisha clothes, as I was really into Japanese people."

Morrissey was quoted of *Kimono My House* in *The Quietus* in August 2010: "In a glorious surge of deserved success in 1974, the very comprehensive lyric sheets accompanying Sparks' albums prove that Ron Mael is clearly driven to tell, yet he answers the media by skilful quietism and by impersonating various walls. Ron Mael is an undoubted genius, and where else would a true genius live but in the catacombs of hell? Ron asks his younger brother Russell to sing the words — in chilling falsetto. Russell sings in what appear to be French italics, and has less facial hair than Josephine Baker. It is a scream, because the songs are screams... Who on earth would write a pop song in such a way? A song about an arts and crafts competition where 'lovely Claudine Jones/has to come to push her quilt', but where Tracy Wise gets a prize. There is no category for this madness — except the category of madness, and Sparks are only let down by their name. At fourteen, I wanted to live with these people, to be — at last! — in the company of creatures of my own species."

It seems that Morrissey's enjoyment of Sparks started from a young age. One Steve Morrissey from Manchester had his reader's letter printed in *New Musical Express* in June 1974: "Today I bought the album of the year. I feel I can say that without expecting several letters saying I'm talking rubbish. The album is *Kimono My House* by Sparks. I bought it on the strength of the single. Every track is brilliant — although I must name 'Equator', 'Complaints' and 'Amateur Hour' and 'Here In Heaven' as the best tracks, and in that order." (In the same feature, another reader's letter stated: "Sparks are the biggest sound since flexi-discs. *Kimono* is a great record. Heavy vibes, babe. A mantle-piece.") The admiration is mutual though. Russell was quoted of Morrissey in *The Guardian* in October 2002: "He's one of the few musicians we have contact with, and we admire what he's done. He's succeeded in creating his own persona without having to copy anyone, and he's stuck with it."

Smiths guitarist Johnny Marr was quoted of 'This Town Ain't Big Enough For Both Of Us' in *The Know Magazine* in December 2016: "There's nothing better than commerciality crossed with an interesting mind." Thurston Moore of Sonic Youth also included the single in his list of all-time favourite songs in *Consequence Of Sound* in January 2014.

When asked how they felt about the fact that so many other artists (New Order, Depeche Mode, The Human League, Erasure, Kurt Cobain, Thurston Moore and Bjork) enjoyed Sparks' music, Ron was quoted in *Loud And Quiet* in July 2018: "There's an ambivalence to how we deal with that. Obviously you're happy that something you're doing is something somebody else thinks is special enough to grab a hold of in a small way for them. But when those bands become commercially successful and you hear large elements of what you've done in that, to be honest there is a certain amount of jealousy about that. We try and shove that aside. You just move on, you don't fixate on that too much and become bitter and paralysed." When quoted in *LA Weekly* in November 2018, Russell noted that it is a "diversity of bands that we know are Sparks fans" and that "it's not all coming from one era."

Justin Hawkins, of The Darkness fame, recorded a cover of 'This Town Ain't Big Enough For Both Of Us'. Sparks approved of this. Russell was quoted in *The Scotsman* in September 2005: "Justin plays all the instruments himself and the drumming is really impressive." The brothers even made an appearance in the promotional video for the track. Of all the falsetto voices in rock, Justin Hawkins' certainly does the song justice, technically and artistically.

Upon being asked, "Your influence has a wide reach – everyone from The Darkness to Depeche Mode over the years. Is it any easier to be Sparks in 2017 than it was in say 1977?", Ron was quoted in *Diffuser* in September 2017: "I think there's more acceptance of what we're doing, less questioning of where we fit in. Sometimes it borders on the amazement of some people that we're still doing this with some passion, so just the admiration of stamina some people show. I think it's easier in the sense that what we're doing now is being accepted in total, at least by a certain audience. There've been times in the past we've had to kind of focus on one era or even one country's knowledge of us, but now we can kind of present ourselves in our totality so it's kind of easier being what we are, which is the sum of everything. It's also been easier in a sense because we've had the experience of late of working in the film area which really rekindled a passion for coming back to working in a more traditional song structure. In the past when we tried to kind of reinvent ourselves, it had to still be done within three and four minute songs, and that would involve either trying to find a producer who could alter how you were doing things, like Giorgio Moroder, or trying to do it on our own somehow, reinventing things with *Lil' Beethoven*."

Ron was quoted in *The Guardian* in August 2017: "When we started it was only for the fun. We never had any thoughts of legacy or anything like that. It was a thrill to have one album released. Music was only a fun thing to do for us, I was studying graphic design and Russell film – but it gradually became something more than the other stuff." And what a legacy it is!

Having such a phenomenal discography is perhaps something of a double-edged sword for some artists. On the one hand it is an achievement in and of itself, but on the other, it creates a situation where, to an extent, any new work is always going to be compared to older works that fans hold dear. Russell was quoted in *Loud And Quiet* in July 2018: "There are a lot of times that I think if we were judged solely on the music and not also on the fact that we do have a history, that we might be embraced more strongly in a commercial sense. I don't think our music sounds like it comes from somebody who has a long history, necessarily. In a larger and more commercial sense it makes it more difficult for us, so in a way we wish we could see what would happen if we were a new band presenting the *Hippopotamus* album for the first time." Either way, Sparks are still on a journey of creative exploration and long may it last. Ron was quoted in the same feature: "What we do is expansive enough in its scope to be used in ways that aren't just necessarily three or four minute pop songs. We're going to continue to see how far we can push Sparks."

Throughout their career, Ron and Russell have worked hard. A combination of staying motivated and having a good working dynamic seems to have kept them going, and constructively so. Russell was quoted in *The Independent* in September 2017: "There's a daily routine, and we're pretty methodical about it. We have a work ethic. Ron shows up on time (to Russell's home studio) and well groomed. People say 'what do you guys do the rest of the time?' but we pretty much don't do anything else. It's a full-time job. Having had so many albums now you have to keep pushing yourself to come up with things that excite yourself and ultimately you hope are going to excite our audience and a new audience. And that is a bigger goal. We approach things thinking if someone had no clue about Sparks is this going to be striking and relevant?" Ron was quoted in the same feature: "Part of the thing is we have a common vision of what we should be doing. And we have such different roles in what we are doing. I have no desire to be the vocalist. I have the keyboards and the writing. So we don't kind of feel unfulfilled in the collaboration."

Ron was quoted in *The Scotsman* in September 2005: "For better or worse we're willing to work without any kind of input at all. We're in contact with other people who offer to listen and give their opinion but we are so insecure working this way that we don't even want to know if what we're doing is wrong because that might shift the direction. We don't want someone else's opinion and we're prepared to accept the consequences. We still have a faith and idealism about music: that you can challenge and do something eccentric and bold but also accessible. That's what keeps you optimistic about your future."

Ron was quoted in *Northern Transmissions* in 2018: "One thing that we're really fortunate to have, some people see it as a burden, is a sensibility that runs through everything we do. That's there all the time, so the desire to keep going is trying to morph our ways into different contexts. We have the advantage of the two of us being the nucleus of what we do, so we're able to enter different landscapes without worrying if it sounds like a band, or other concerns. The vitality of things comes through working in different formats, and working with a few amazing producers that have inspired – Tony Visconti, Giorgio Moroder and Todd Rundgren. Now we've been working as of late without a producer, but we've retained what we've learned from them. Now we're trying to see how far we can push things within the context of our sensibility. It gets harder and harder, but we have the freedom to work in the way that we want that other bands might not have." When asked if he and Ron had fought, Russell was quoted in the same feature: "I think it's only creative issues, and it's related to the big picture. They're not that significant, you discuss certain sounds or whether the chorus should be repeated a second time. On the bigger issues, there's less friction." Ron was quoted: "It's kind of a reflection of how our roles are separated and defined. It takes the sibling rivalry out of things that would break up the band."

Russell was quoted in *Exposed* in August 2017: "We take pride in the fact that we don't rely on the past. People could be listening to us for the first time, or this next record could be the first album they ever hear by us and we need to make it worth their time. We approach every new album in that kind of way. We are not lazy, we are motivated. We just hope it is as exciting for our audience as it is for us... We fight against the status quo and what pop is, or rather people's perception of what pop should be. People write lyrics that are like bland wallpaper – unassuming and boring. We think that lyrics should be something stylistic at least. As an artist you have a blank canvas, you can do anything you wanna

December 28, 1974   SOUNDS   Page 7

Tweeter In Woofer's Clothing

"The only point we're trying to prove is to have a buzz ourselves... wasn't a cause for us to get popular."

do. It seems like there are people that prefer the ones that sort of fit in with a movement. For Ron and I, it has always been an 'us against them' thing. We always like to think that there is a 'them' we are rebelling against, and we do that with our music, our lyrics and our image."

*****

It is impressive really, that despite being famous for over forty years, there is very little known about Ron and Russell Mael. Their biographies state where they come from, what sports they liked playing and a discography of fascinating albums. Nothing is known publicly about the brothers' personal lives. Personally, I would argue that the cult of celebrity too often overshadows the importance of the music itself and that the Mael brothers have done well to reject that trend; they are known for their music and not their personal lives. Not many other musicians, even of a similar age, have managed to maintain such mystique. There are a few exceptions such as Bob Dylan, but still.

Russell was quoted in *The Independent* in September 2017: "Well we're in good company with Bob Dylan. But we always think that what we do with our music should be the thing and live performance and what you see on our album covers. We think the whole story of the music and the image and how we portray ourselves is more compelling. We feel the less you do know it keeps the mythology and the image in a better position. You do know about us in the type of music and the lyrics and their sensibility. Through that you do know something about our lives." Ron was quoted in the same feature: "I would be happy presenting our albums as part of a joint autobiography." In response to the interviewer's question of "But you wouldn't even say if you have partners for example?", Russell was quoted: "The vagueness is more interesting than the reality."

Conversely though, there is certainly a sense that the brothers put something of themselves into their stage performances. The journalist noted of Ron in *Sounds* in December 1974: "Off stage Ron looks more relaxed, although his eyes still intensely scan all around." Russell was quoted in *Exposed* in August 2017: "A lot of people wonder if we are the same type of people offstage, and our onstage personas are basically an extension of how we are in real life. Ron is a severe kind of person and you will not confuse him for anyone else. If you see him you will know he is Ron from the band. It's because who we are on stage is a projection, a larger-than-life image of who we are in real life – but I think it's not too much of a stretch for the imagination." Russell was quoted in *Sounds* in January 1975: "We just really like to base what we're doing around our songs and around our personalities so that there's not any extraneous things so that the real focus is on the songs and around us 'cos I think there's enough going on in the song. I don't know if we'll have any gimmicks. We *are* the gimmick!"

It comes across that Sparks have always been both forward thinking and comical; an intriguing combination of seriousness and humour. If so, it has probably served the Mael brothers well throughout their career. They have often been quoted in a way that suggests they are objective about their work without losing their sense of humour. When asked if they listened to their old material, Ron was quoted in *Sounds* in September 1974: "It tends to make you too selfconscious of your career. In ten years' time I'm going to get all of our albums and listen to them and have a real wild time." I swear that Ron is pure comedy! A serious sentiment soon turned into something silly and unexpected. Brilliant! When Pete Makowski mentioned that he had read the lyrics from *Kimono My House*, Ron was quoted in *Sounds* in June 1974: "Sorry to hear that." Makowski replied: "You don't like them?" to which Ron was quoted, "Oh! Oh like them, no I shouldn't have interrupted." Funny guy.

Ron Mael has moments of pure hilarity to this day. In an interview with *The Scotsman* in September 2005, this journalist relayed a conversation that he had with Ron: "'As a child, I was rather disturbed by you, Ron.' 'And you could be again', he says, shooting a resonant look." In the same feature, the journalist stated: "Meeting Sparks has its hazards for a journalist because when the brothers are bored, they tell massive fibs. When they had just arrived in Britain, they persuaded one reporter that they didn't possess the necessary work permits and had been forced to record their album on a Dover to Calais cross-channel ferry. In another interview they claimed Doris Day was their mother – 'We only said it once and now it's in our official biographies', says Russell." What pranksters! Russell certainly has his moments too. He was quoted in *The Scotsman* in September 2005: "Ours is a less obvious relationship conflict than Ray and Dave Davies or the Oasis brothers. They just punch each other."

Whilst the Mael brothers had their reasons for pranking the media, like many good jokes, there have been times when it has backfired. Russell was quoted in *The Times Magazine* in March 2003: "All kinds of stories got fabricated along the way. I think it came about in England in the seventies when we had done so many interviews all asking the same thing, and so we thought we ought to spice it up a little. So we were child actors, catalogue models and all that – but we didn't have that background to be honest." To which Ron was quoted: "There seemed to be no reason why we had started doing the music, so we started making up these lies." Russell was quoted in the same feature: "We were Doris Day's sons for a long time too. In fact, in German pop lexicons, I'm listed as Dwight Russell and he's Ronald Day. We once went to Scandinavia and the publisher for Doris Day tried to contact us, thinking we really were her sons, because there were some royalties due from the publishing. So they said we could come by the office in Stockholm to collect the money and we said 'to be honest, morally, we cannot do that.'"

The Mael brothers humoured Pete Makowski when he asked them if they were still planning on opening a restaurant. Ron was quoted in *Sounds* in June 1974: "Oh, we'd really like to. That would just be another side of what we're doing. We'd be kinda catering to a need within ourselves, to do something with a bit of excitement about it." To which Russell was quoted: "Not a Wimpy type place, a bit more classy." And more food rumours from Russell regarding a cookery book: "Oh, 'Munching Meals The Mael Way', yeah, that'll be coming out in the fall."

It's entirely possible that Sparks weren't trying to be deliberately comedic through music though. Ron was quoted in *Melody Maker* in November 1974: "I don't write funny songs, I like things where it's really blurred, and you can't tell if it's funny or not funny. I think mystery is a good thing." He was quoted in *Sounds* in June 1974: "I really don't like songs that are just comedy records. I think that there should be something more to it. The whole dividing line between something that's funny and really sad is really fine and a lot of times you can't tell what the situation is at all or else it could be both. It's the same with people as well." Russell was quoted in the same feature: "There's a definite lack of bitter sweet songs. I think a sort of controlled confusion is good. If things are too clearly defined as to what is happening it is kinda, I don't know. I like not exactly to know what somebody's getting at, not exactly know what emotion is coming out. That's the type of film that I like. When you see a trailer for a film they usually say 'the comedy of the year' and we found that with one film called *Morgan, A Suitable Case For Treatment.* And in the States they said '*Morgan* – the laugh filled comedy about a loony', and things like that. And we saw it and it was a really sad movie."

I'm really glad that somebody asked Ron this question because it's probably one that a lot of people have been curious to know the answer to. In an interview with *Sounds* in December 1974, he was asked about how does he "manage to keep up such a rigor mortis like expression?" and doesn't he "ever feel like bursting into a fit of laughter?" Ron was quoted: "Occasionally when there's a pile of about twenty-five people on stage, then that really strikes me as funny. It's just a case of gawking at people and they gawk back. But things happen sometimes that are funny, that in a way surprise you. I've had shoes, various brassieres and other undergarments thrown on stage."

As much as all other musicians who worked with the Mael brothers are an important part of Sparks' legacy and what the band achieved creatively, endearingly there is a large part of Sparks' story that is about two brothers who have a phenomenal working rapport with each other – even in a world where the media interest might have been overwhelming for them as individuals. In an interview with the *Daily Mirror* in July 1979, Russell was quoted as he explained why Ron was going to be quiet: "He wouldn't talk to you anyway, because he is extremely shy, introverted and finds it difficult to communicate with people. He is rather intellectual but a bit of a weirdo. I get on with him very well, but then I understand him."

Ron was quoted in *The Times Magazine* in March 2003: "I collect things, it's like a disease. I collect sports figurines, which is a bad thing to collect because they take up so much space. And I collect Beatles trading cards – and I've always bought a lot of records, although I'm not what you'd call a record collector. Also, when I was little, I used to go to all the automobile shows because I loved cars, and so I've got a collection of all the new automobile launch brochures going right back." Russell added that his brother also has over a thousand snow domes.

A big shout out to all the Sparks fans reading this book. Eccentricity is awesome because it fuels creativity and individuality. Russell was quoted in *Sounds* in June 1974: "Whatever you're doing you should do it well and with conviction and we approach each thing and do it the best way we can do it." If a few more people were willing to take the innovative leaps that Sparks did in 1974, and indeed throughout their career, then maybe the world would be that little bit less boring. As it is, a massive thanks to Sparks for putting their music out there and adding a little bit more colour to the proceedings. Weird is good. Stay eccentric. Stay innovative.

The Recordings

Kimono My House

Personnel

Sparks
Russell Mael – vocals
Ron Mael – keyboards
Martin Gordon – bass
Adrian Fisher – guitar
Norman "Dinky" Diamond – drums, percussion, castanets

Technical

Muff Winwood – producer
Richard Digby-Smith – recording engineer
Tony Platt – recording engineer
Bill Price – mixdown engineer
Nicholas de Ville – art direction, cover concept
Ron Mael – cover concept
Karl Stoeker – photography
Bob Bowkett, CCS – artwork

Track Listing

All tracks are written by Ron Mael, except where noted.

Side One
1. This Town Ain't Big Enough For Both Of Us (3:05)
2. Amateur Hour (3:37)
3. Falling In Love With Myself Again (3:03)
4. Here In Heaven (2:48)
5. Thank God It's Not Christmas (5:07)

Side Two
6. Hasta Mañana Monsieur (3:52)
(Russell Mael, Ron Mael)
7. Talent Is An Asset (3:21)
8. Complaints (2:50)
9. In My Family (3:48) (Russell Mael, Ron Mael)
10. Equator (4:42)

*****

Island Masters bonus tracks (1994)
11. Barbecutie (3:07)
12. Lost And Found (3:19)

21st Century Edition bonus tracks (2006)
11. Barbecutie (3:07)
12. Lost And Found (3:19)
13. Amateur Hour (4:44)
(Live at Fairfield Halls, Croydon, London,
9th November 1975) (Features the
Indiscreet line-up of Sparks)

Side Three – 40th Anniversary Edition (2014)
11. When I Take The Field On Friday (2:45) (1973 Demo)
12. Barbecutie 2:56 (1973 Demo)
13. Windy Day (3:46) (Ron Mael, Russell Male)
(1973 Demo)
14. Marry Me (3:07) (1973 Demo)

Side Four – 40th Anniversary Edition (2014)
15. A More Constructive Use Of Leisure Time (3:37)
(1973 Demo)
16. Alabamy Right (2:27) (1973 Demo)
17. My Brains And Her Looks (3:13) (1973 Demo)

Propaganda

Personnel

Sparks
Russell Mael – vocals
Ron Mael – keyboards
Trevor White – guitar
Ian Hampton – bass
Norman "Dinky" Diamond – drums
Adrian Fisher – guitar

Technical

Muff Winwood – producer
Richard Digby-Smith, Robin Black and
Bill Price – recording engineers
Bill Price – remix engineer
Monty Coles – concept and photography

Track Listing

All tracks are written by Ron Mael; except where noted.

Side one
1. Propaganda (0:23)
2. At Home, At Work, At Play (3:06)
3. Reinforcements (3:55) (Ron Mael, Russell Mael)
4. B.C. (2:13)
5. Thanks But No Thanks (4:14) (Ron Mael, Russell Mael)
6. Don't Leave Me Alone With Her (3:02)

Side two
7. Never Turn Your Back On Mother Earth (2:28)
8. Something For The Girl With Everything (2:17)
9. Achoo (3:34)
10. Who Don't Like Kids (3:37)
11. Bon Voyage (4:52) (Ron Mael, Russell Mael)

*****

Island Masters bonus tracks (1994)
12. Alabamy Right (2:11)
13. Marry Me (2:54)

21st Century Edition bonus tracks (2006)
12. Alabamy Right (2:11)
13. Marry Me (2:54)
14. Interview - *Saturday Scene* 8/11/74 (7:16)

Sparks 1974

206

Tour Dates

December 14th 1973 – London – Marquee
December 21st 1973 – London – Marquee

June 20th 1974 – Cleethorpes – Winter Garden
June 21st 1974 –   Hull – University
June 22nd 1974 – Leeds – University
June 23rd 1974 – Cheltenham – Town Hall
June 24th 1974 – Birmingham – Top Rank Suite
June 25th 1974 – Lancaster – University
June 26th 1974 – Swansea – Top Rank Suite
June 28th 1974 – Redruth Cornwall – Flamingo
                          Ballroom
June 29th 1974 – Taunton – County Ballroom
June 30th 1974 – Torquay – Pavilion

July 2nd 1974 – Plymouth – Mobile Theatre Home Park
July 3rd 1974 – Bristol – Victoria Rooms
July 4th 1974 – Dunstable – California Ballroom
July 5th 1974 – Cambridge – Corn Exchange
July 6th 1974 – Southend-on-Sea – Kursaal Ballroom
July 7th 1974 – London – Rainbow Theatre

November 2nd 1974 – York – University
November 3rd 1974 –   Newcastle – City Hall
November 4th 1974 –   Leicester – Montfort Hall
November 5th 1974 –   Liverpool – Empire
November 6th 1974 –   Bristol – Hippodrome
November 8th 1974 –   Reading – University
November 9th 1974 –   Exeter – University
November 10th 1974 – Coventry – Theatre

November 11th 1974 – London – Hammersmith
Odeon
November 13th 1974 – Swansea – Brangwyn Hall
November 14th 1974 – Oxford – New Theatre
November 15th 1974 – Blackburn – St George's Hall
November 16th 1974 – Lancaster – University
November 17th 1974 – Stoke-on-Trent – Victoria Hall
November 18th 1974 – Southport – Theatre
November 19th 1974 – Edinburgh – Odeon
November 20th 1974 – Dundee – Hall
November 21st 1974 – Glasgow – Apollo Theatre
November 22nd 1974 – Manchester – Free Trade Hall
November 23rd 1974 – Hastings – Pier Pavilion
November 25th 1974 – Torquay – Princess Theatre
November 26th 1974 – Bournemouth – Winter
Gardens
November 27th 1974 – Birmingham – Town Hall
November 28th 1974 – Dunstable – California
Ballroom
November 30th 1974 – Paris – Olympia

December 7th 1974 – Amsterdam – Concertgebouw
December 8th 1974 – Rotterdam – Doelen
December 11th 1974 – Zurich – Volkhaus
December 15th 1974 – Brussels – Forest National
December 20th 1974 – Leeds – Town Hall